THE CROWN IS MINE

Takeover Season

Part II

THE CROWN IS MINE

Takeover Season

Part II

Warren Holloway

Table of Contents

Chapter 1

"Keisha come down here! We have to go!" TK yelled out from the bottom of the steps, after the call between him and Red Rain ended. Suga Baby came down quick, hearing the urgency in his voice coupled with him using her government name. Her heart is beating fast, seeing the look on his face. "What is it?" "Them mutha fuckas snatched Shandrea up!" TK responded, saying Red Rain's real name. The deep, painful, sinking feeling came over her making her weak, angry and helpless all at once. She sat down on the steps, eyes watering, filling with tears, in fear of losing the one female she loves. "They wanted her alive, or they could have killed her easily in the car. This means they want something in exchange". TK said, trying to comfort Suga Baby with hope. " Give them whatever they want. I need her back here with us". Suga Baby said with a broken voice. "I'm a give these Spanish niggas more than what they ask for, disrespecting what we have. We going back up north, to bring her home. We'll connect with the hommies Little Ki Ki and Trappa-D, set them straight before we fly out. Then I'll reach out to a few people, to make sure we have what we need when we land". " If they hurt my bitch, I'm a kill all of them mutha fuckas". Suga Baby said angered, emotionally crushed by this situation, especially the thoughts of harm being done to Red Rain. "Let's go, we don't want to waste time, that could be valuable in saving her". TK said taking Suga Baby's hand, leading the way out of the crib, tuned into avenging his girl's girlfriend, so she can come back home to the family they have. Meanwhile, up north in Harrisburg, PA. The Latin Kings are driving into the South Side projects, also known as the South Acres. A death trap for those who aren't welcomed, especially with the sixty plus rows of project housing, allowing shooters multiple avenues to get away or leave the unwanted, in the large green dumpsters if need be. The Latin King soldiers pulled into the projects where the Latin Kings control all drug movement and gang activity. As they pulled up, Red Rain can see dozens of Spanish niggas and bitches spread out, strapped, some trapping, others playing dominos, some on the grill cooking, some looking out for cops, fiends, and unwanted traffic from gang rivals, the rest drinking beers, enjoying their position as ranking gang members. They exited the car, keeping Red Rain at gun point walking her to one of the stash houses they run and secure. "Amor de Rey". "Siempre". The gang members exchanging greetings, saying: A King's Love. The other responded: Forever. Loyal gang members that are willing to die, representing the crown. "Oye, quien es eso?" The gang member playing dominos asked. He looks to be the ranking member of those here, having lookouts on both sides of him. "Don Rico wants us to hold her". The gang member Tito responded. The block boss nodded for them to continue on. They did as instructed taking her to the stash house. Red Rain taking in her surroundings in case she gets a chance to find her way out of this tight situation, with all of these gang members around. She was also impressed with the amount of security and organization these Latin Kings have, locking down and securing this project. She never seen anything like this down south. She was concerned how she would find her out, with this level of organization and security. Always thinking, she would try her best, either way, she's ready to die trying. They came up to the stash house with two Latino goons standing in front visibly strapped, boasting the Latin King crown tattoos on their arms and chest. " Ella es para Don Rico". Tito said. They waived them through, into the house. Tito and the other goons with him, leading Red Rain into the house. Once inside of the house, Red Rain can see in the living room, goons counting stacks of money, from the different products they move, ranging from molly, ecstasy, heroin, and cocaine.

This is one of many money houses in this project and city. There is also two females present, with guns on their waist line, along with Mac 11s draped over their shoulders. The older female having this dark stare as if she's seen her fair share of murder and hard times. Her short black hair, heavy makeup trying to preserve her youth, looking older than forty five, from all the alcohol and cigarettes she consumes. The older female is also the one looking to be in control of all taking place inside of this house with the bags of money being counted. The younger female slim built, not to be taken lightly, her hair long with braids, not to look cute, to stand her ground and position in this dominate gang of men. Only twenty years old having put work in already in another state, getting her bones, killing a correctional officer that disrespected a Latin King boss behind bars. "Take her up stairs, put her in the back room. You stay with her until someone comes to take your place. The rest of you, get back out there". The older female directed Tito and the other street soldiers, clearly showing her position of power. They followed her instructions, knowing anything less would be their demise after humiliation. Tito took Red Rain upstairs. " Sit over there. You try to run, I will shoot you. If you somehow get out of this room, without my permission, they will shoot you. Either way, you're not going anywhere until Don Rico says so". Tito said gripping his gun, staring intently at her, attempting to establish ground rules, as if Red Rain really gives a fuck. If she can find a way out, she definitely going to take it, and leave a body count in her wake if need be. "You better hope Flaco don't die chica, or you die of a violent death. Flaco is Don Rico's sister's son". Tito added. " I don't fear death like you bitch ass gang members that came into my spot, trying to get at me. I should have gave folk the green light on all you bitches". She responded, referring to having Duttaman shoot them all, leaving no witnesses or chance of retaliation, like now. Tito sat gritting his teeth, flashing back to the situation at the house, when Duttaman had the drop on all of them. His day could have easily ended right then. "Too bad Don Rico wants you alive, or I would unload this whole clip into that pretty face of yours, right now!" Tito responded offended by her statement. "You a pussy, a flunky, that's why you're sitting up here with me, and not down there counting or getting to the real money". Red Rain said taunting him, getting under his skin with her words of truth, not being scared of her position of capture. "Fuck you puta!" Tito snapped, jumping up, smacking Red Rain across the face with his gun, making her fall onto the bed. "Who's a pussy now bitch?!" "Tu es stupido cabron! Que le pasa a ti?" Doña Tulia, the older woman that was downstairs asked when she came up stairs hearing the commotion. Tito turned seeing the dark stare and disappointment in her eyes. She asked Tito if he was stupid and what's wrong with him for acting the way he is. "Tu tiene un trabajo, and you're fucking it up". Doña Tulia added, making him aware he only had one job to do. Doña Tulia, the capo of the Pennsylvania Latin Kings, overseeing the state's money laundering to the home land and heads of the gang. She answers to Don Rico. " Lo siento jefe". Tito stated apologizing for his actions. "Don't be sorry just do the job that is asked of you". She responded looking at Tito then over to Red Rain as she continued speaking. " If she has to use the bathroom, the door stays open, so you can see her at all times. If she's hungry you feed her like she's your guest. You'll also treat her like your guest, until you're told to put a bullet in her head, or let her go, entiendo?" "Si jefe". Tito responded, nodding his head in acknowledgement. "What's your name nena?" Doña Tulia asked. "Red Rain". She responded. Doña Tulia's eyebrows shifting, trippen off of her stripper name. "Are you hungry?" "Yes", Red Rain said knowing there may not be too many windows of opportunity to eat with being in this position, awaiting her fate. "I'll have food sent up. Anything else you need within reason, he'll get it for you". Doña Tulia said, before making her way out of the room, back downstairs. At the same time her cell phone sounding off, getting her attention. She see that it's Don Rico calling. " Hola que tal?" She answered. "Amor de Rey". "Siempre, que pasol?" "Tu tienes la morena?" He asked if she has Red Rain with her. "Si ella esta aqui". She responded letting him know she's here. " I'm coming that way now". "Esta bien". She responded allowing him to know she's good with that. She ended the call continuing down stairs to make sure Red Rain gets her food, since this could be her last meal. Within fifteen minutes Don Rico arrived coming into the house. All inside stopping what they were doing to formally greet their higher ranking boss. Then they headed up stairs with the four goons Don Rico was travelling with. Tito stood from the chair he was sitting in, greeting Don Rico. Don Rico focused on Red Rain, getting straight to it. " Word got back to me that you may be the one that downed mi hermana en sangre. A Latin Queen?" Don Rico said referring to La Reina. Red Rain was eating the fried pork chop, before they entered the room. She cleared her mouth before speaking. "I didn't kill anyone here in Pennsylvania. I came for business only. Now your goons came at me earlier, trying to take what's mine, so I protected it". Red Rain said standing her ground on her actions. Doña

Tulia respecting her gangsta as a female boss. " My Latin King brother told me you and your team took out La Reina, then you pop up supplying a large portion of the city, even our customers". Don Rico paused looking over at Tito. "Oye adonde ella's telefono?" He asked where is her phone. Tito removed the phone from his pocket, handing it to Don Rico. He held the cell phone in front of Red Rain's face unlocking it. Then he checked her last dialed number, calling it. Someone picked up, staying silent until Don Rico spoke. "How much is she worth to you?" Don Rico asked, wanting to really get to the persons responsible for killing La Reina. TK also having the phone on speaker, allowing Suga Baby to listen into the call, along with Trappa-D and Little Ki Ki. "She's worth the earth you step foot on". TK responded. Red Rain deeply warmed by his response, knowing he would do whatever it takes to get her back safely. " Sangre para sangre hermano". Blood for blood, Don Rico responded, then added "You killed a member of our organization, then you had this puta come into this city, like she's the new queen. There is no honor in this level of disrespect". Don Rico stated firmly, upset, yet ready to set a example out of her or anyone attached to what took place with La Reina. " Give me the phone". Suga Baby said, taking the phone allowing her emotions to get involved. "Where she at?" "I'm right here Suga Baby". Red Rain yelled out, wanting her to know she's alive and breathing. " We'll give you money, a million cash to let her go". Suga Baby said. "I have money chica. I tell you what I don't have, your respect to offer me money in exchange for the life

13

you took, in killing La Reina". " I'll lay down my life for hers, and you still can keep the money". Suga Baby said wanting to protect Red Rain. "When will you come to make this possible?" He asked calmly, wanting to honor La Reina, with blood for blood, avenging her. "Today, right now, I'll fly up". "Call this number when you get here. If you don't, she'll be dead by sunrise". He said ending the call, handing the phone to Doña Tulia. "Llamame por la tarde, or when they get here". "Amor de Rey". "Siempre". As he exited, TK and Suga Baby moved quick, heading north thinking ahead, to make sure everything turns out in his favor.

The Crown Is Mine

Chapter 2

Harrisburg International Airport. TK and Suga Baby landed, exiting the airport being greeted by TK's Pittsburgh hommies he did a bid with up state. Real Crip niggas that was doing time for putting that work in. The Crip hommie Tre, light skinned with a bald head, full beard cut close. A real G nigga with a gangsta swag and stroll, rocking his black jeans, black tee, with a blue bandanna hanging from his left pocket. The Ray-Ban shades concealing Tre's eyes. Tre also having his Crip set inked on his arm. "What up cuz?" Tre said seeing TK coming through the door. Tre came four cars deep, ranging from the Dodge Magnum, Charger, Impala, Audi A6, all with young Crips ready to put that work in. They're standing by their cars, scaring some of the passengers exiting witnessing the sight of the many young black thugged out goons looking all too serious. The old school Impala was just him and his right hand man Wheezy, a short nigga with braids, dark skinned, full beard cut close, thick eyebrows, skinny, but never to be taken lightly. He did a bid for shooting it out, plus banging out with the cops when they tried to pull him over, when he was fifteen. He got certified, they slapped him with a 20-40 year bid. He came home pissed at the world, now he's a OG in this

15

Crip shit, just like the hommie Tre. "What's good my nigga? Good looking on coming though in the clutch. I'm a definitely bless you so you can look after your team". TK said greeting the hommie Tre and Wheezy. " Coast to coast we Cripping. I got niggas in this city too if we going to war". Tre responded. "I want to get baby girl back, at the same time, let these Latin King niggas know even if I'm not around, this is my city". " You already know cuz niggas be trippen, we got that steel for y'all too". Wheezy said as they got in the Impala, passing them two modified 9mm with thirty round clips. "That's for you and lady cuz, to pull up like what's cracking? They going rock out or roll with it". He added.

Both TK and Suga Baby appreciating the modified heat. "No safety, plus the triggers on them is super light cuz. You squeeze a half a dozen in one squirt cuz. We all roll with one in the chamber on everything. Seconds cost lives when niggas be trying to be on that movie shit cocking guns for effect at the last minute". Wheezy continued. " Time won't be wasted if they hurt my bitch". Suga Baby said gripping the 9mm. TK called up Red Rain's cell phone as previously instructed by Don Rico. It's close to 9PM, Doña Tulia noticed checking her watch as the phone started ringing. She picked up figuring it has to be the moreno calling for Red Rain. "Hola". " I'm in the city, ready to secure business. Where do you want me to pick her up at?" TK asked allowing them to know he came for Red Rain, even if this is not their intention, it's his and Suga Baby's, by any means necessary. "South Acres, Spanish Alley. When you get here, park your car, then call back". She responded. This allows the female boss to have the area secured, having all eyes on him when he pulls into the projects. She ended the call, leaving him to figure out his next move. His strategy to get Red Rain back alive and well. Within twenty minutes from the airport, they made their way into the South Acres projects. Not as originally planned. TK, Tre, pulled up in the Impala, while Wheezy as instructed by the big hommie Tre, looked after Suga Baby, also on standby with the rest of the goons, who were in proximity of Spanish Alley, where all the Latin Kings had look outs and the hood on smash with all of the drugs they push. Soon as Tre parked the Impala, they noticed two Jeep Grand Cherokees pull up. The doors opening allowing Don Rico to exit with his team of Latin King brothers. " You know we get out, ain't no turning back, especially seeing how these clowns got shit on lock". Tre said being gang affiliated, having his hood secured, but not like this. This layout is all controlled by them in every aspect. Even while TK and Tre are in the car contemplating their out, the Latin King soldiers, were made aware of their presence and to be on the look out for them. "I can't leave baby girl to die. That would be disrespect to me and Suga Baby. Niggas would think they can come at me and my team. That shit is not an option my nigga, so I'm going in to get her". TK said, taking hold of the phone calling the number. Doña Tulia picked up. " You better be here or your friend will die, with holes in her pretty face". Doña Tulia stated ready to expedite this process now, with Don Rico present. "I'm here where you said to park. You bringing her out here or what?" He questioned, trying to figure out what's their angle. She hung up relaying his presence to the other soldiers outside. They closed in on the Impala with guns at the ready. Both TK and Tre ready to rock out right now, thinking they were lured into a trap. "These bitch ass niggas is nobodies. We shoot them, we ain't going get baby girl back". TK said trying to bring calm back to both of them. " These clowns don't want no real work". Tre said gripping his fully modified Mac-11 with a hundred round clip. "Stay in the car, I got this. If you don't see me or baby girl in fifteen minutes, give your team the green light to wet all of these mutha fuckas". TK said stepping out of the car, following the Spanish niggas to the crib in the middle of the row. Soon as he got to the front of the crib, two goons stood outside protecting it. They searched TK finding the modified 9mm. " You came for war hermano?" The Latino asked looking on at the gun then back up at TK. "War? If this was war, you would be dead already, because you would never see me coming". TK responded. "Fuck you cabron!" He snapped waiving them into the house. When he entered the house he seen the money being counted, along with plenty of goons and guns. Doña Tulia gesturing for him to go up stairs. This eerie feeling came over him came over him, almost like he's walking into a death trap. Red Rain being dead already, Don Rico wanting to avenge La Reina. His reign is over ending right here, leaving behind Suga Baby to take over everything. TK is thinking and feeling as he took each step heading up the stairs. Once at the top of the steps, he can see men standing in the room.

Doña Tulia shoved TK in the back with her gun, to keep him walking forward to the room of Latin Kings. "Where she at?" TK asked. The goons in front turning towards TK's voice, parting so he can come in. Don Rico sitting on the bed beside Red Rain, with a gun to her head, the hammer pulled back on the black steel .44magnum snub nose. "Hermano, I see you showed up, and understandably so, with her exotic beauty, the ride or die demeanor. She's a valuable asset to you, maybe more". Don Rico said. Red Rain not even scared at this very moment. For her, it is what it is. " Where's the cabrona that was talking over the phone, willing to exchange her life for this one?" "She couldn't make it, so I came instead to get her in exchange for the money we offered along with a new distribution deal of grade A product. This is my gesture of respect for your loss". TK said having approached this situation with a chess strategy, with multiple outlets, to prevent from being checkmated, which would mean his violent demise. " This isn't about money or distribution hermano". "You want blood? Then point your gun at me. I'm a tell you something I learned from La Reina. Insurance, is the most valuable thing in this business". TK said removing his cell phone, seeing that Don Rico isn't going to negotiate for money or cocaine supply. "You kill me or anyone connected to me, no one under the Latin King umbrella in this state will be safe". TK added as the phone stop ringing when La Vieja picked up. "This better be important, I was in the middle of something?" La Vieja said being entertained by a male and female, having their way with her.

19

Part II

"I'm calling in that favor I told you about". TK responded. " Put whoever thinks they're in charge on the phone ". She said referring to Don Rico. She already did her research on him once TK brought it to her attention, that he has a problem with him. Don Rico took the phone wondering who is on the other end, and what value does it have to this current situation. "Quien es ese?" Don Rico asked who is it. "La Vieja, the original, not to be mistaken for anyone else. You're disrupting my business with your emotional antics. My associate by now has offered you money and distribution. You should take it and let bygones be just that, gone and out of the way of our business. Either way, no harm will come to my associates. I have great financial interest in both of them. I don't think you or your gang can afford it or the amount of blood I would crave for, to call us even". La Vieja stated firmly. Don Rico like most people in this underground world of crime, has heard of the notorious cartel capo, her violent ways including the power that backs her. The most recent act, having Rolo and Coco Brown decapitated, their bodies hung upside down from the bridge in Atlanta, all to make a statement, don't betray her. Even with this knowledge of her power and position, Don Rico's pride and Latin King loyalty isn't allowing him to bite down, humbling himself, in letting these two go. " Perdoname La Vieja, these two cabron's killed a ranking member of my organization. In this business it's blood for blood". Don Rico expressed. "Tu abuela Maria Dominguez, she still baby sits for you when you're running around like now right?" La Vieja taunted, already having goons sitting on Don Rico's grandmom's house awaiting her to give them the go ahead. Don Rico loving his grandmom and kids, he didn't want to risk them being killed over this, when he can try to get at them later. He lowered his gun, then tossed the phone back to TK. "Get these maricons out of my sight now!"

The goons lowering their guns too, as they escorted Red Rain and TK out of the house. TK put the phone to his ear. "Whatever you said it worked, making him stand down. I appreciate you". " No hermano, now you owe me a favor when it is needed". She responded, before hanging up to continue her intimate session. TK turned to the Spanish goon that took his gun as he entered the house. "Give me my gun nigga". He passed the gun to TK, before they all walked back to the car. " Rain you lucky you get money, the sex and excitement between us is good, otherwise I would have left you back there". "I love you too TK. Plus Suga Baby wouldn't let you leave me and you know this". She responded smiling walking in front of him switching her ass, giving him a visual of what he also loves as much as Suga Baby. Red Rain knows he loves her just as much, because she is a ride or die, loyal chick, along with a freak in the bed, adding the excitement to his and Suga Baby's relationship. " Tre you can call off the hommies. Like I said I got you for this, even though them little niggas you got, came to put that work in". TK said. "It ain't shit cuz, we still might catch wreck if we catch any of them fools slipping on our way back to the city". Tre said, as they drove off to link back up with Suga Baby and the other Crip hommies. The level of excitement between Suga Baby and Red Rain was high, having thought they would never see one another again. As they embraced with kisses and hugs, Tre's little hommies was taking in the visual of these sexy bitches, kissing caressing, happy to see one another. At the same time TK was making plans to bless Tre with money and product all on the strength of his loyalty holding him down. He also wanted to make sure he keep real niggas like this on standby, as long as he's in this game...

Chapter 3

A few days later, Little Ki Ki is at OLG a soulfood spot owned by famous female R&B singer. She was with her girlfriend Karin, spending a little quality time, also talking about the future of their relationship, and life outside of the street life. "What's on your mind babe?" Karin asked, seeing this look on Little Ki Ki's face as she's eating her food. "Ain't nothing, but some hood shit. I'll figure it out. Right now I want to focus on us, and that dress you stacked in, that's begging me to take it off". Little Ki Ki responded, shifting the attention and mood from herself back to Karin. This made Karin light up smiling inside and out, being appreciated. " I got dolled up for you as always ". Karin said, licking the barbecue sauce from her fingers. " I found a place we can call our own". She added, knowing Little Ki Ki wasn't about to live in her old crib having memories of her exes. She wants something new, that they can call their own. "You ready for that? Meaning my schedule, lifestyle and seeing me every night, even when you wake up?" Little Ki Ki questioned, as she wiped her hands, taking hold of her fresh squeezed lemonade. "I'm sure, but it sounds like you're not. I figure if we do this, shifting the state of our relationship to something comfortable and real. You'll let go of that other life to focus more on me and the future of this real estate empire, we'll build along side of this love we have". Karin stated, looking into Little Ki Ki's eyes with love. Wanting her to be onboard with this change, this next level of life and love. Little Ki Ki is smart enough to know the street life isn't going to last forever, as much as she loves the power and money that comes from her position in the game. She also knows that Karin, is the best thing that ever happened to her and for her. What they have together is beyond sex. They have love for one another, backed by a vision of business, and a emotional future of promise. " Babycakes, I'm in on this with you, this new crib thing. But first I have to sever ties with this life, so it doesn't lead to our door step, or taint our real estate business". Little Ki Ki said as she bit into her chicken and waffles, allowing Karin to process her response. Karin now drinking her ice tea with lemon, taking it all in. Then she expressed her views. "How long will this process be? Because the property won't be on the market for long". Karin questioned with concern, yet wanting to have a time line to entertain. Especially, with her being a calculated and precise individual, wanting to have control over her own destiny, including all around her. Little Ki Ki also picking up on this. " Show me this property that got you excited". Karin took her phone accessing the pictures, accompanied by a walk around video of the five thousand square foot home, boasting four large rooms, each with full bathroom. The master bedroom on the second floor opening up to a large balcony, with a over-view of the four acre property, with a in ground pool and cabanas. The space and design luring Little Ki Ki into the idea of this being her home. "I know that look, you really like it. This could be ours, breaking in every room, even find ourselves in the cabanas, getting drunk off of Hennessey and each other". Karin said with a smile, thinking about the future with this woman she loves. "Buy it". Little Ki Ki, matching her excitement. "I'll handle this side of business, so we can make that house our home". She added, ready to tie up loose ends, calling it quits. She knows when to fold her hand in this game. "I love you for thinking of us babe. Not being selfish or allowing the streets to take more of your attention and love than I do". Karin said feeling this moment of happiness. Little Ki Ki got up from her side of the booth, coming over to sit next to Karin. "Nothing or no one has my heart or attention like you do". Little Ki Ki expressed to her as she leaned in, finding her soft lips.

This kiss seeming more explosive, with emotions running high between the two of them, as the sacrifice for their relationship is being made and understood. Little Ki Ki's free hand sliding up Karin's body fitting navy blue dress, parting her legs, finding her place, rubbing up against her jewel of passion through her panties. Karin's heart is beating fast, knowing they're in a public place, which is turning her on even more, having the feeling of being watched and or caught in the act. Either way, she welcomed Little Ki Ki's touch, as she slid her panties to the side, allowing her fingers to find her pearl along with the other finger strategically placed inside of her. Karin's moans vibrating over Little Ki Ki's tongue, loving the feeling at the same time, she knows this can't continue, with her being a loud moaner and screamer when the intense orgasms starts rushing through her body. So she halted Little Ki Ki's play. "Mmmh babe, you know I'm loud. Plus you know you'll make me super soak messing this dress up". Karin said knowing how turned on she gets with magic touch. Little Ki Ki obliging, removing her fingers, placing them to Karin's lips, allowing her to take them in. " I just wanted you to know how much I appreciate all of you". She said removing her fingers from Karin's mouth, then added. "Let's get out of here, so we can finish this show on the road". They did just that, exiting the restaurant, making their way out to Karin's pearl white Porsche truck, with light tint, black rims giving the truck a sexy racing look. Little Ki Ki noticing two white males in a car roughly a half a block back. It caught her eye because they stood out in the Crown Victoria. She jumped into the truck with Karin, not saying anything about the two men, only watching in the side mirror, noticing they just pulled out. Now Little Ki Ki's mind and heart are racing, thinking to herself. Is this the feds or local drug task force following them? I move quiet, not drawing being all flashy and shit. How the fuck they get onto me? She's thinking watching the Crown Victoria pick up speed, trying to keep up with the Porsche truck, as Karin jumped on the high way to head to her place. Close to ten minutes later, the car was still following them. This is not good. Little Ki Ki is thinking. "Karin, don't go to your house. Them folks is following us in that Crown Vic, a few cars back. Jump back onto the highway.

Fuck man!" Little Ki Ki snapped, her mind going into overdrive, processing her out to evade these fools. "I got this babe". Karin said as she made a abrupt u-turn shifting directions to shake the tail. When she turned around she stared intently at the passing car, getting a good look at the two men inside of the Crown Victoria. They were also caught off guard, realizing their cover was blown. " Drop me off close to the hood. I have to get shit under control". Little Ki Ki said, knowing it couldn't have been her drawing the attention. It's her flashy ass hommie Trappa-D, always wanting to be in stunt mode, having the little niggas in the hood following behind him. They made it to the hood, a few blocks from where the trap house is. "Be safe babe and keep the focus so we can get away from this life. Remember my love awaits you and only you". Karin said giving Little Ki Ki a kiss, which is the only good thing in this moment of being pissed off with thoughts of being compromised, and tailed by the law, whoever it is the feds or local task force, it's not good for her or business. " I'll call you when I take care of these fools that's putting the spotlight on this thing we doing out here". Little Ki Ki responded closing the door throwing up the peace sign as Karin drove off.

Chapter 4

Little Ki Ki was walking a few blocks from the hood, having had Karin drop her off away from the hood, not wanting niggas in the hood to see who she fuck with, so they don't try to snatch her up, using her as leverage, to get at Little Ki Ki. As she was walking, so many thoughts are racing through her head, at the same time her head is on swivel checking her surroundings for the law and jack boys. She was also thinking the feds may be still searching for leads on the crooked ass federal Agent Budda Sanchez's death. She finally made it to the hood turning the corner into the trap, seeing the flashing red and blue lights, unmarked cars and local police in synch snatching the hommies up that was out on the blocks getting paper, all pinned down on the ground or up against squad cars, being frisked. She even seen Trappa-D gripped up against his new truck. She froze in mid stride, knowing she can't continue forward. She stood at the top of the block looking down the street, watching this all unfold. Even the DEA agents coming out of the stash spot with bags of money, cocaine prepackaged, broken down to twenties, dimes and nicks, paraphernalia, digital scales. Trappa-D noticing the hommie Little Ki Ki at the top of the block, hoping she takes off running, to get away, instead of the entire team going down. He will take this for her, no matter what. She turned around quick, walking fast adjusting her Yankee fitted, before taking out her phone hitting up TK, to put him on point. He picked up on the second ring. "What's good with you?" "Burn the hommie Trappa-D's number, them alphabet boys just snatched him up in a raid on the block". Little Ki Ki said angered by it all. TK didn't panic with her association to Trappa-D. He views Little Ki Ki as a rida, a real street figga, that will honor the street code until her last breath. "Say less about it. You good?" He asked. "Yeah I'm a fall back til I see what time they on, or if the coming my way, ya feel me?"

"You ain't alone out here little hommie. I got you, no matter what you need". TK said. "I need to get away for a little". "I'll send Suga Baby your way. Go to the chicken and waffle spot, around the corner from your hood". TK responded before hanging up, making his way into the bedroom where Red Rain is laid up in being catered to by Suga Baby, changing her bandage on her leg. "Aye yo, the little hommie Trappa-D got snatched by the feds. I need you to go scoop Little Ki Ki from the chicken and waffle spot around the corner from her hood". TK said. "You sure she ain't trying to play a nigga?" Suga Baby questioned wanting to protect her family. Meaning her, TK and Red Rain. "That little bitch is more gangsta than most niggas. She ain't break-ing for no one". Red Rain chimed in, knowing how Little Ki Ki roll, having seen her around at the club before. " Pick her up, take these keys to Red Rain's crib up north. She'll lay low up there, for now. Tell her to dump her old phone, get a new one at the airport. Soon as she get it, tell her to holla, we'll go from there". TK said looking out for Little Ki Ki, at the same time his mind is working, thinking about how this opportunity has presented itself for change, that was needed for Red Rain, keep her close, after the situation popped off with the Latin Kings. TK is figuring to have her in position, while using Red Rain's contacts, allowing her to still benefit. Right now the north is too dangerous for Red Rain, especially with the emotional interest TK and Suga Baby has in her. "She better be there or I'm not sticking around to be watched". Suga Baby said being paranoid, and rightfully so, with all that has been going on lately. " You good Rain?" She asked. "I'm good baby go take care of Ki Ki". "One more thing". TK said looking over at Red Rain. " When Little Ki Ki gets settled in, all of your clientele will go through her, so you never have to step foot in PA. I don't want to risk losing you or going to war with them Latin King mutha fuckas. We'll send Little Ki Ki all she needs to hold her down". TK said. Red Rain surprisingly nodding her head agreeing with him, especially not wanting to be put in a position she was in, with crazy ass Don Rico. "We'll find someone down here to hold ATL down. When our surroundings change, we flow with it, or stay ahead of it". TK added, before tapping Suga Baby lightly on her ass as he came up on the side of the bed, where her and Red Rain is. She got up, blowing each of them a kiss before making her way out to pick Little Ki Ki up. On the

31

other side of ATL, Little Ki Ki made it to the hood chicken and waffle spot, going inside placing a order to take out. She did this so she can hang out inside, not standing out front looking like she plotting on the joint. As she was waiting on her order, she was looking out the window, seeing multiple cop cars and federal agents' cars rolling pass with what seem like the whole hood that was under her and Trappa-D. She even seen Trappa-D in the back seat of the fed car, accepting his fate as a hood boss should, when you're as flashy as he was. It didn't take long before Suga Baby pulled up in her rose gold Audi A7 tinted windows, black rims, a real bossy look that's not too flashy. Little Ki Ki already knowing to toss her phone in the trash, so she did that while she was inside the chicken and waffle spot. Suga Baby lowered the window, so she can see that it's her, since she had never seen this new whip. Little Ki Ki nodded her head, getting into the car. "Aye shawty, good looking ya feel me? You want some chicken and waffle for ya troubles?" Little Ki Ki said, extending the bag of food. Suga Baby took it, not having it in awhile, plus she was craving for that combination. "Shit got crazy for your team huh?" Suga Baby asked as she pulled off. "Them fools wanting to be poster boys for the drug game, like this shit legal out here". Little Ki Ki responded. " We got a spot for you up north, plus we getting you new phones. One for up there, plus one for you to hit us up directly. Everything you need will be in place". "I ain't trying to be on no longer term shit up there ya feel me? My shawty down here, plus I got investments in this city, ya hear me?" "Nothing is set Ki Ki, this is all to put you in position getting this money nonstop, while staying away from this city until shit cools down for you and your team". Suga Baby responded. As they're on their way to the airport riding on the highway. Little Ki Ki noticed a Porsche truck the same color, make and model as Karin's. The closer they got she also took notice to the two men that was following behind her in the car, when they left the soul food spot. Karin standing outside of her truck looking to be arguing with the agents. They was probably wondering where Little Ki Ki vanished to. Little Ki Ki not liking that her woman was put in that position. This made it even more clear, that it's time to bow out of this game, before it knocks on her door step, forcing her to lose it all. They will be watching Karin, to see if they can track Little Ki Ki, not unless Trappa-D takes all of the weight, directing the attention and their focus on him. Even so, they couldn't get Little Ki Ki directly with anything, because she been fell back on the hand to hand shit, leaving that to the little hommies. Little Ki Ki put her head back, closing her eyes taking it all in, losing the hommie Trappa-D who is like a brother to her, along with money and product, she'll have to pay TK with, out of her own pocket. Ki Ki knowing she has to stay ahead of this situation before it takes her under. Right now she'll head up north, where no one knows her, stay low and always steps ahead to be preeminent in this game, until she's ready to bow out of it.

Chapter 5

A month after the raid on the block with Trappa-D and the little hommies in the hood. The hood was officially experiencing a controlled drought. TK didn't want to rush, sending product into a hood that was hot like that. He did have Red Rain reaching out to ATL niggas to prep them to be in position to take over that hood. Red Rain was also holding down the north, through her social media platforms, also with Little Ki Ki, finding her way. No one tried to test Little Ki Ki as they tried with sexy ass Red Rain. Her thugged out demeanor spoke volumes. Little Ki Ki got respect from the YG niggas too, who showed her around the city, hoods, clubs, best spots to eat, even the secured Latin King hood. She took it all in, thinking her plans through, while stacking paper. This time around, she didn't have to break it down. Everybody Red Rain sent her way, was brick customers only. Little Ki Ki copped a summer bike, nothing flashy, a plain 750 Katana all stock. It allowed her to get around fast on the low, wearing her helmet, concealing who she is. Little Ki Ki is now taking a ride through the different parts of the city, Uptown, riding through Duck Down Ave, seeing this hood buzzing getting money. Her focus is locking down the entire city, along with the surrounding cities.

This level of power she's feeling and having with less exposure she had back in Atlanta. She's really embracing this new position. She rode her bike through Moore Murder, checking out what was going on in this hood. She peeped the lookouts, movement, trapping on the low, along with the young shooters tucking weapons under cars, staying close by in case shit pops off. She left the Uptown area heading to the P-Funk, a large project between Uptown and the Hillside. It has one way in, and one way out. Dangerous for law enforcement, having had multiple cop shootings, from the rows of project homes. Soon as she entered the P-Funk, all eyes was on her, presence with the look outs, checking for cops and fiends coming into the hood. These thugged out niggas had guns and product stashed in chip bags, under cars, close to the dumpster, or inside of abandoned cars. All things that would be overlooked by an outsider. She noticed a few nice cars, classics, tricked out with candy paint, gold rims with spokes. All old school whips, Cadillac, Lincoln, and Chevy Impalas. Little Ki Ki noticed a food truck along with a ice cream truck. This visual is summer to her, bringing back memories of growing up in the hood back in Atlanta. She pulled her bike up, flipping the kick stand down, hopping off the bike removing her helmet. Her dreads freshly twisted with bees wax. She walked up to the food truck with the smell of French fries leading the way, coupled with spices and barbecue. "Say man, let me get the fries with that barbecue pork on top". She asked having scanned the menu hanging on the outside of the truck. " You want anything to drink with that?"

The heavy set, bald head nigga serving the food asked. "Orange Crush". She responded as she discretely scanned her surroundings, seeing how they running shit out here. She noticed these young niggas ranging from ten to fifteen years old, hanging around the truck. " Y'all little niggas want something off the truck?" She asked the young bucks. "They good". The big man inside of the food truck responded on their behalf. Little Ki Ki cut her eye up at him. "It's not a problem folk, I'm paying for it". She stated. At the same time one of the young bucks exited the truck, running over to the parked Nissan Altima. She spotted a white female in the driver's seat. The young buck didn't have any money in his hand. " Here you go bruh ". The big nigga said handing her the food. She handed him a twenty. " Keep the change in case the little hommies want something later". She responded, making her way to her bike where she stood enjoying the food while checking out the scenery, watching how they operate.

She stood looking on at the young bucks running the money to the ice cream truck, while the product came out of the food truck. It's smooth and clever, especially keeping young bucks in rotation, however when this shit goes bad, it's going to go down hard, because kids are involved. What a person gets for killing someone is what he would get if caught with a few rocks. It's like getting caught on school grounds or selling product within a thousand feet of a school. "Say man, you change up your style, you can have a fleet of food and ice cream trucks throughout the city and state". Little Ki Ki said. He picked up on her southern accent, at the same time, didn't know who she is, so his paranoia kicked in. " I don't know what you talking about bruh". He responded, trying to brush her off. At the same time a chrome custom painted 79' Chevy Nova pulled up with fat tires, chrome rims, white interior, piped with chrome. Little Ki Ki turned towards the bass dropping on Young Dolph's song Blu Boyz, featuring Snupe Bandz. Everyone around nodding their head to the anthem. It's the YG nigga Bundles, with his goon hommie Duttaman. "Yo what it look like? I see you fucking with them fries". Bundles said. " You already know folk, they special ya feel me?" She responded, indulging into the fries. Bundles looked at big man in the truck, then back to Little Ki Ki. "That's all you came for right? You know that's my peoples?" Little Ki Ki looked up at the fat nigga with a smirk. "Make sure you give the young niggas some of them fries, they earned it". She said dumping her trash in the can on the side of the truck. Then she tossed up the peace sign. " Stay focus out here ya hear me?" She said hopping on her bike, taking off racing out of the P-Funk. Big man inside the truck realizing she was the plug. Most would overlook her just as he's done. This is her intentions to never be seen or figured out, while making the money and staying in power. What more can she ask for.

Chapter 6

"Oh my God bitch!" Suga Baby yelled out from the master bedroom bathroom. "What?" Red Rain asked as she muted the TV watching her day time stories. Suga Baby came out of the bathroom over to Red Rain, bringing into view a positive pregnancy test. Red Rain's eyes widen, her heart beat picked up in excitement. "No, you serious? I'm going to be a Godmom or aunty?" She asked, trying to figure her title in the baby's life, at the same time extending her hand to rub Suga Baby's belly. "Hey in there, you better be a girl, so we can go shopping together". Red Rain said full of excitement, before leaning in kissing her belly, since Suga Baby is only wearing bra and panty. Red Rain standing up from the bed to hug her girl with love. " Are you happy, because you're not saying anything?" Red Rain asked. "I'm scared and happy all at once". She responded, stepping back to further explain her emotions. " I'm still on the run. How can I deliver this baby without them knowing who I really am? I don't want anything to happen to our baby". She said connecting to the idea and reality of her situation, rubbing her own belly now, feel like a mother to be. "Don't trip, we having this baby. We going to be just fine. You ain't going to jail, especially if I'm around. We'll have the baby delivered here if we have to. I love you bitch, I'm really going to love this baby, spoiling her". Red Rain said. Suga Baby started laughing hearing Rain keep saying a girl. " You're crazy saying it's a girl. You know TK is going to want a boy to be his little thugged out twin, so he can be rough with". "He got us for that rough stuff". Red Rain said being funny, then added, " Now let's go tell him so we can see his face of being a daddy". They made their way downstairs to the lower level of the home designed like a sports bar and night club. TK was having a drink watching Sports Center, watching the commentators debate on who is the best between Jordan, Lebron and Kobe.

Suga Baby stood in front of the 60 inch wide screen TV dancing and rubbing her belly, before she started singing. "We having a baby. We having a baby. You're going to be a daddy". " I hope it's a girl, so we can go on shopping sprees". Red Rain added. TK finished his double shot of Hennessey, standing up coming over to both of them, pulling them close, as he spoke. "This changes everything". He said kissing Suga Baby's forehead as he placed his hand on her belly. " Is that a good or bad change?" Suga Baby questioned, still having mixed emotions and fears. "Good, meaning I don't want to bring my child up in this life we're living. We have to stop before the baby gets here. Invest our money to keep a steady flow of income". TK responded. " I don't think quitting is an option in dealing with La Vieja". Red Rain reminded them. "She don't control us, we control our own destiny. We made it this far. It's up to us to bow out with respect, so we can raise my son inside of here". TK said making her feel secured by his decision, even if La Vieja didn't agree with it. " Babe we all step down leaving the business to Little Ki Ki, while reaping the benefits getting a percentage of sales, since she'll supply all of our clientele". Red Rain suggested thinking ahead like a boss chick, removing themselves from the day to day operations. "That's why we love you Rain, you always bossing it up". TK said giving her a kiss on the lips. "Mmmh, you want to practice getting me pregnant, so our babies can grow up together?" Red Rain said being funny and real at the same time. "We definitely can afford it". He said looking on at the two ride or die women he loves and would kill for. "You want it right now baby?" Red Rain asked TK, turned on by the thought of having his baby. Her hand reaching down touching his manhood. Her soft touch bringing him to full attention. Suga Baby caressing his chest, getting in the mood, ready to celebrate with explosive intimacy. TK's cell phone started ringing, shifting his immediate attention from this erotic session that was about to take off. The only person with this direct line is La Vieja, so when it rings he doesn't hesitate to stop everything to answer it. What made him really focused, he never sent word for new business, so something must be wrong. Red Rain lightly biting her lip in heat, turned on wanting him to fuck her all day, leaving his babies inside of her. TK answered his cell phone. "What's good?" "Hermano, we need to talk". " You want me to fly down to Miami?" "No, I want you to come out front. It's important". She responded hanging up the phone. His heart is beating fast, as his mind is racing trying to assess this unexpected visit, especially since she told him once before he wouldn't see her in person unless there is a problem. What could it be? He's wondering. " Suga Baby stay here, Rain get your strap and stand at the front door. La Vieja is out front. She wants to holla at me". "I'm pregnant not dead. I refuse to stand by or in the background as long as I can squeeze a trigger". Suga Baby stated, running upstairs to put some pants on, before grabbing a Tek-9 with a fifty round clip, out of the money room. Red Rain taking the AK-47 propping it on the side of the door as she stood in the door way. TK walked over to the four truck convoy, where he was patted down before entry. Once inside the truck the convoy pulled off allowing TK and La Vieja time to talk serious business. " I have a problem that needs to be taken care of immediately. Call it a favor for a favor". La Vieja said getting straight to it, looking over at TK. "Whatever it is I got you. You came through for me and my team when I needed it. I can do the same for you". TK responded, being just as serious as she is, at the same time displaying his loyalty for her in this business. She puffed on her cigarette stressed, blowing out a cloud of smoke, at the same time handing TK the eight by ten manilla envelope.

"Open it to see what it is you'll be needing to take care of". She said. He did as instructed, removing the contents inside of the envelope, sliding the eight by ten photos out. The first of the photos is a split level home, real nice look-ing. This made his eyebrows angle, wondering why a pic-ture of a house? The next photo making it more clear. It's a picture of a white male, around forty five, military style haircut. The man is hugging up with a brunette that has dimples and a radiant smile. " That's Federal Agent Brian Tucker. They have five year old twin boys, Brian Junior and Bret. Agent Tucker is the one responsible for turning Rolo and Coco Brown, who as you know set me up. He's also leading the continuing investigation that I need to end with his death". La Vieja said as TK continued to look through the photos, seeing the twin boys with bright blue eyes, innocent smiles, no worry of the world of trouble their father has put them in. "Just him, not the wife and kids right?" TK questioned, not really a fan of killing kids who have no part in this adult business. Plus he wasn't too fond of killing law enforcement that is on the straight path, unlike crooked ass Federal Agent Sanchez. "Kill whoever is in your way of getting him. Whatever you do, don't fucked this up, or it will not be good for any of us". She stated firmly, knowing a botched hit on a federal agent, would put the underground world on lockdown, until answers are produced. " Say no more. I'll take care of it". TK responded, seeing the address on the envelope. He couldn't say no to her, even if he wanted to. He's bound by this life, his loyalty to her and this business. He wanted the power the day he came home from up state. Now he has the position of power that demands more than he ever expected. "Once this is done, be ready to take over the entire east coast, with tons of cocaine shipments that will come. You and your team will also be a part of this increase with lower numbers to crush any competition". La Vieja said. Giving TK encouragement to follow through on taking out this federal agent. So many thoughts running through his mind, Suga Baby just telling him she's pregnant. The conversation they all just had about bowing out of the game. Now this contract that must be fulfilled, pulling him back into this business and position of power. The convoy of trucks pulled back up to TK's townhouse. Suga Baby and Red Rain still standing there on point awaiting his return. The convoy stopped in front of the townhouse. " One more thing hermano. In seventy two hours I have a preliminary hearing. I don't want that puta or his family showing up". La Vieja said, with a murderous look in her eyes, not caring about Agent Tucker's wife or kids. All of this adding even more pressure with this time line being closer than he expected. Meaning he has to act fast, checking out the area and how he's going to have this taken care of. "No worries, it's done. I'm on it soon as I get out of this truck". TK assured her. She nodded her head dismissing him, allowing him to exit the truck, making his way back over to where Suga Baby and Red Rain is. Each of them can see the look on his face that it's something heavy weighing on him. " What's wrong baby?" Suga Baby asked as he came up the steps entering the house. "She want me to cancel this mutha fuckas contract on life". He said removing the pictures. Suga Baby and Red Rain looking on at the photos. " Awe these little boys are cute. I hope she don't want you to hurt these babies?" Suga Baby asked. "Her main focus is him". " Who is he?" Red Rain asked. "A fed nigga, that's trying to take La Vieja down. I have less than seventy two hours to get this shit done. Right now I need a mutha fucking double shot, to think this shit through". He said walking away to get his drink. Suga Baby and Red Rain, knowing this situation from both ends, won't turn out as anyone expects, whether he kills the fed or not.

Chapter 7

After two days of plotting, planning, TK sent Suga Baby and Red Rain to Agent Brian Tucker's house, posing like they're a interested couple, seeking a home in the cul-de-sac. They were also checking the area to see if any of the homes has security systems, Ring door cameras or outside cameras. Most of the homes were equipped with door cameras. He thought ahead having the women go in to soften the wife through conversation, especially seeing these two well dressed females, that pulled up in a snow white Maybach truck. Elisabeth Tucker had the day off, to spend with her twins who are now in the back yard running around. She already had been introduced to Suga Baby and Red Rain, when they came yesterday with a realtor, using their real names, pretending to pay all cash for the home across from her house. Elisabeth was also captivated by the affection these two females are showing one another. This is something they didn't have to fake. "Keisha, Shandrea, I really admire what you two have. It seems like after the boys were born, my husband doesn't display this level of affection that got me pregnant in the first place". " He should be all over you Elisabeth, especially for bringing those two cute boys into this world". Suga Baby said. "I would be all over you, babies or not".

Red Rain added trying to make her feel good about herself, at the same time this compliment is making her lower her guard. She started blushing at the thought of being catered to by a woman. A thought that never crossed her mind, until now. " So where is your husband now, so we can give him a few lessons on how to cater to you, appreciating you more". Red Rain asked. "He's at work. He's one of those DEA agents. He should be home soon". She responded looking at her watch. " Well we don't want to overstay our welcome, besides you'll be seeing more of us soon. We'll invite you over for drinks and excitement". Suga Baby said. Elisabeth's mind racing to naughty seductive excitement with these two women. She didn't realize she was turning herself on, as her legs pressed together to control the urge, stimulated and forced by her thoughts. Elisabeth cleared her throat, finding the words to respond. "Well, you don't have to go. I don't have to cook dinner tonight, we're going out to a Tai place I love. The boys love the Tai rolls". Elisabeth said being nervous with the thoughts of being close to these women as they are with each other. She hadn't been intimate in almost a year. It's not like it use to be with her and Brian. He's always exhausted from work. " We'll keep you company for a little while. We see you don't talk to Karen much, I can tell the way she looked at you yesterday". Red Rain said. "She's just rude. Can I get you ladies anything to drink, soda water?" "What type of alcohol you have?" Suga Baby questioned. Red Rain looking at her, then her belly. "She'll have a bottled water". Red Rain said. " Would you like some Grey Goose? My husband loves that stuff when he comes home after a long days work". "He should be loving you just as much". Red Rain stated. Elisabeth being naive allowed her heart to be open to her husband to the point she forgot about herself. She came back into the living room with two shot glasses, the bottled water for Suga Baby, the Grey Goose for her and Red Rain. She poured the drinks handing Red Rain the glass. She took it at the same time, allowing her fingers to caress Elisabeth's hand. This soft sensual touch, triggering her thoughts of seduction with a female. Truthfully, she yearned to be touched by anyone right now, to unleash all that she's been keeping in. She downed the shot only to refill quickly. Red Rain did it again, caressing her. Her touch tweaking Elisabeth's curiosity. " You have this look of curiosity. It's ten times more erotic, explosive than you imagine. We as women, know what our bodies desire". Red Rain said looking on at Elisabeth. Her lips parted allowing heated breaths to flow over them, as she's entertaining thoughts of allowing a female to explore her body. Red Rain came over to the couch Elisabeth is on, she took her hand pulling her to her feet. "Relax, allow my touch to be welcomed by your body". Red Rain said, caressing her hair, down to her neck, trailing over her 34A breast. Her breathing picking up, not having been intimate or having any touch in some time. Red Rain's face coming close enough to hers, she can feel the warmth of her flesh being near. Her hand running the outside of her pant over her pearl. She leaned in, finding Rain's lips, her hands wrapping around Red Rain, as Rain slipped her hand into her

47

pants, finding her close shaven playground, parting her vaginal lips working her magic fingers. Her moans vibrating over Rain's tongue. Suga Baby enjoying watching her work. Elisabeth is so turned on feeling the sensation building up racing through her body so fast, this touch is way more stimulating than her husband's touch. Red Rain found her spot working it. Her moans intense unable to hold them in. " Aaaah, aaaah, aaaah, I can't believe this, aaaaah, aaaah, aaaah". Her legs shaking, as the intense flowing is escaping her body with sensational satisfaction. Red Rain removing her fingers placing it in Elisabeth's mouth, she didn't resist caught offguard. Then she quickly gathered herself having a flush look on her face, still turned on. "I just heard a car door shut". Suga Baby said. " Oh my, I hope that's not my husband". Elisabeth said wanting to experience more, even both of the ladies at the same time, exploring her body, uncovering hidden treasures of pleasure. She was sounding disappointed that it was her husband. Red Rain looking at Suga Baby, ready to shift their entire demeanor to gangsta bitch mode, handling the business they came for. The front door opening as Brian came into the home, Elisabeth greeting him with false happiness as if she's glad to see him right now.

"Hi honey, how was your day?" She asked leaning in to kiss him. He closed the door behind him, before looking on at the two women in his home. Also the kiss his wife gave him, tasting like her when he gives her oral. Even though it has been awhile he's been down on her, he knows her body. "What's going on here?" He asked, now seeing his Grey Goose on the table. "You don't even drink, and you're giving my shit away to strangers?" "No honey, these two are buying the house on the other side. I'm so excited to welcome them as our new neighbors. They're a nice couple like us honey". Elisabeth said trying to explain. " Nice or not, they shouldn't be drinking my vodka, you too". He said walking pass them heading to the bedroom, to get ready to take her out tonight. "I'm sorry ladies. I didn't think he would be like this. You have to go for now". Elisabeth said. Suga Baby removing a silenced Glock 9mm from her handbag. Red Rain also having a silenced Glock she removed. Elisabeth seeing this, froze in fear and confusion, since her body was still processing the sensation and flow. Now this abrupt act of danger is present, allowing her to know she's been deceived in the worse way. She started shaking in fear for her children and husband. " Please don't kill me, my boys need me". She pleaded. Red Rain raising her index finger up for Elisabeth to be quiet. Suga Baby headed to the bedroom where Brian went. She came up to the door that was closed. She turned the knob slow trying to sneak up on him. Soon as she entered the room she can see all of the clothing he was wearing on the floor, leading to the shower. She closed in on the bathroom, gun out in front of her ready to put work in, killing this federal agent. Suddenly, a force from behind her knocking her in to the wall, dazing her. It's Agent Brian Tucker. He faked being in the shower to deceive these two females in his house. One he recognized from the Wanted posters for murder in PA.

He recognized Suga Baby from the wanted poster, so he lured her into the room knowing they didn't come to buy any house. His instincts paid off, or he would be dead right now. "Rain! Help me!" Suga Baby yelled out in fear, quickly regaining her bearings. Right then, it sent Red Rain into overdrive, shifting to beast mode squeezing the trigger on Elisabeth sending a couple slugs slamming into her flesh, sucking the life from her before she hit the floor. At the same time as she was falling to the floor, the twins came into the house from the back sliding door, calling out to Elisabeth. "Mommy I'm hungry". Soon as they came in, Red Rain snatched them both up by the collars. " Stop you're hurting us". Brian Junior said. "I'm a do more than that, if your dad hurt my bitch!" "What's that?" Bret questioned in fear and confusion. "I got your boys! If you want them to live, you'll let my bitch go!" Red Rain said. "You're both going to jail for coming into my home!" "We'll take our chances with that. You got five seconds to let her out of there or your boys will be playing with these bullets in their face!" "Rain! He's calling for help!" Hearing this, there was no more negotiating, she released the twins, only to pump a round into the back of their heads, before rushing into the bedroom unexpectedly, gun out. Her fast movement making him release Suga Baby, shifting quick having his cell phone in his left hand, pistol in his right hand. Rain unleashing the full clip as she's charging towards him. Each slug finding his face and body over and over, thrusting him up against the wall, before his body slid down lifeless to the floor. Suga Baby jumping up, taking her gun firing two more anger filled rounds into his body. "Damn, that shit was way too close". Red Rain said. " I'm a burn this bitch down!" Suga Baby snapped, angered by what happened. They rush back down the steps getting what's needed to set a fire, that would leave no trace of their presence.

Chapter 8

A few days later up north, Little Ki Ki was on her motor-cycle coming from dropping a brick off to the hommies in the Duck Down Ave area Uptown. She chose a nigga Peanut, cause he stay low getting to it. He also did a bid back in the day for putting in work and getting that paper, so he wasn't about to be flashy drawing on himself. Plus he had all of the young bucks in the hood holding him down, while he reap the benefits of being a hood OG. Little Ki Ki was riding down the street where her lay low spot in the Bellevue area on the Hillside is, away from all the high traffic of the hood. As she was coming down the street she noticed a nigga standing outside of her crib looking around like he was up to something. No one knew where she lived, she didn't operate like that. He came up on her porch knocking on the door, still looking around, before discretely removing a .357 magnum. Whoever he is, isn't aware that she's the one riding the bike, with her having the helmet on, or he didn't know she be on the motorcycle. She popped her bike up on the curb closing in on her crib. At the same time the impatient nigga thrust his foot into the door with the thoughts of robbing for drugs and money. Little Ki Ki halted her bike, turning it off as she jumped off flipping the compartments open, that's concealing her twin snub .45 Black Eagle automatics, hosting ten slugs in the clip, one in the chamber ready to rock out. She entered the crib, removing her helmet, closing the door behind her, so no one else thinks this is a free for all. Whoever this nigga is, he's determined and must have either been tipped off to her spot, or he was just watching her or the crib. Either way, he's about to pay for this level of disrespect, testing her gangsta. Little Ki Ki heard this stupid nigga up stairs talking to himself, trying to figure out where the money or product is. The product wasn't here, it' at another spot. The cash she kept in the basement in laundry bags underneath dirty laundry, propped up by the washer and dryer. She crept up the steps with both snub noses out in front leading the way, her fingers inside of the trigger guard, close to the trigger. She followed the sounds of this fool recklessly going through her things, in search of money and product. She entered the bedroom, seeing this idiot had flipped her mattress, now he's in her closest, flipping through her sneaker and boot boxes. He was so focused and comfortable, he sat his gun on her nightstand when he entered the room. She took hold of it before confronting him. "You a stupid nigga, walking into the cage of a beast!" Little Ki Ki said, alerting him to her presence. He turned quick to where he placed his gun. It wasn't there as he'd left it. This sent fear through him, having two guns staring back at him. "What the fuck!? You a bitch!? These niggas ain't tell me I'm jacking a bitch! These mutha fuckas talking about you, like you a nigga!" Hearing him say this, made her aware that some one she knows put this clown on to her, not knowing what he was getting into. "Get on ya knees nigga". She said, wanting to find out who sent him her way. He stared at her as if he's not about to bow down to her. His face frowning up, suddenly, he charged towards her trying to get his gun off of her waistline, to no avail. She took the butt of her gun slamming it into his face, buckling his legs, making him stagger back. " Say man, you try that stupid shit again, I'll fill ya face up with slugs". She stated firmly, with murderous eyes, staring at him just as deadly as the twin .45s he's facing. He's stunned holding his face, trying to figure out how the hell he got into this position, when he thought he had the drop on the spot. "Who sent you my way?" She asked. He's still trying to hold his tongue not saying a word about it. "You tough huh?" She said firing a round hitting him in the thigh dropping him. Then she closed in on him with both guns allowing him to get a glimpse of darkness and death. It was something in her eyes that all made sense why these mutha fuckas talk about her like a nigga, she's a female goon, that's really about this street life. "Alright bruh, don't kill me. That nigga Fat Jay sent me". He said in fear of what would be next if he kept silent. The name he tossed out didn't register with her. She has no business dealings with no one by that name. " Who the fuck is that folk?" She questioned, ready and wanting to find out to make them also pay for trying to get at her, like she's going to let it fly, because she ain't from around here. "He stay in the projects with the food and ice cream trucks". He responded hoping his life would be spared. Especially with him not expecting his day to end right this moment. Little Ki Ki briefly contemplating if she should let this nigga go, or if she should put him down allowing his death to be the message to anyone in this city trying to test her gangsta. "Get up nigga. I'm going let you live so you can tell that fat piece of shit, he fucked with the wrong G. He want to come for mine, I'm a take all of his!" She stated pushing the stick up nigga out the room down the steps out of the back door. "You come back, I'm a dump both of these clips into ya face, to clear all thoughts of jacking a G like me". She said still aiming her guns at him as he hopped out of the back yard through the gate. Once he was gone, she rushed back into the house securing all of her money, stuffing it into a book bag, before strapping it on. Then she hurried back up stairs making sure she has all the important things that can't be left behind. All the other material things she can buy over. Now she has to leave taking the money to a different spot. She hopped on the bike taking off, thinking about her next move to make Fat Jay pay for this attempt on her. This alone set a raging fire inside of her to make sure it never happens again.

Chapter 9

Within twenty four hours of the botched robbery on Little Ki Ki, she put something in motion that's going to allow her to get revenge while making a statement. At the same time she plans on taking over the projects after this power move she's about to make. Soon as her motorcycle revved up coming through the P-Funk, Fat Jay became alert seeing her coming up on the bike as he's serving customers. Customers he wanted to hurry up and service to get them out of harms way, knowing shit is about to pop off. The nigga that botched the robbery was on crutches coming towards the food truck, until he seen Little Ki Ki jump off her bike removing her helmet, so he turned back around hopping away fast as he could, not wanting to be a part of what's to come. Fat Jay on the other hand, has his eyes locked on her, even with customers placing and getting orders. Little Ki Ki stood to the side of the customers looking on at Fat Jay, with a smirk on her face, taunting him even more with her presence, knowing he fucked up with trying to get at her. "Say man, we need to holla when ya done with these folks. I want them pork fries ya feel me?" She said cutting her eyes over to the young bucks off to the side, that's Fat Jay's runners. Each one taking turns servicing fiends. Once the customers walked away, Little Ki Ki stepped up becoming serious as she spoke. "Greed and stupidity is the downfall of a lot of niggas out here in this game. You could have gotten a blessing if you wasn't so fucking stupid". "Who the fuck you talking to bitch!?" Fat Jay said, bringing a sawed off shotgun into view pumping a round into the chamber. Little Ki Ki didn't flinch, nor was she phased by his actions of having what he thought was the drop on her. She simply adjusted her black Harrisburg Senators Baseball cap, cutting her eyes over to the young thugs on the side of the truck. She nodded her head, giving them the go ahead to move. Right then, the young bucks all strapped with pistols ranging from .380s to 40mms. Thanks to Little Ki Ki, who not only gave them guns but over twenty grand cash for them to split, which is more money than Fat Jay ever gave them. Plus she promised them a connect on the product that will allow them to make way more money than the few hundred dollars a week Fat Jay was paying them. The young bucks rushed inside of the truck with their guns aimed at Fat Jay, making him shift the sawed off shotgun, seeing that they are now the immediate threat to him. He wanted to take them out, all to no avail. The young bucks even if they wanted to hesitate couldn't, seeing the shotgun being turned towards their direction. They squeezed off multiple rounds on Fat Jay sending hot slugs crashing into his large frame thrusting him back, sucking the greed from his flesh as he slammed against the grill his body slumped down in front of. "That's for shorting us on paper nigga". The young buck said also resenting their ex boss.

58

"We good up in there?" Little Ki Ki asked to make sure he was dead. One of the young bucks stuck his head out through the window where Fat Jay once served customers. "Yeah, he down bruh. You still want them fries with pork on it?" The young buck said having no remorse or regard for what they just did. They respect and value the money Ki Ki gave them more. They also fucked with how she conduct herself and business, a real lady gangsta. Little Ki Ki gave a brief smile. "Nah I'm good folk. Y'all need to handle that situation right there. Make sure you keep it tight ya feel me? Y'all be hearing from me soon". She responded tossing up the peace sign before jumping on her bike revving the engine, racing off out of the projects, feeling the power of her position, especially having put this nigga in checkmate for trying to get at her. Those in the street underground life, will respect her gangsta whether they want to or not. Anything less, then whoever think they can test her G, will also meet their graphic demise.

Chapter 10

The next day, down Miami, Florida; Rosanna 'La Vieja' Santiago, her team of lawyers and security are all at the Federal Courthouse, for her hearing for alleged cocaine distribution. The mood in the courtroom is quiet coupled with tension, especially after the death of Federal Agent Brian Tucker and his family. The media coverage, rumors and speculations, linking this cartel style massacre to this case that has currently ran to a dead end. Having its star witnesses murdered along with their heads being decapitated to send a message, making a powerful statement. Now the agent leading the case is murdered, bringing this investigation to a halt. "All rise for the Honorable Judge Smeltzer". The bailiff announced. Everyone stood until the judge sat down. " Are both counsels prepared to proceed?" The judge asked. Judge Micheal Smeltzer, a six foot one, military cut, clean shaven, since his days in the Army. Now having been a federal judge for eight years, he's hard on all criminals that are found guilty in his courtroom. The law in his eyes, isn't meant to be broken, that's why it's set in place. "Your honor, I move to have these frivolous charges dismissed, due to lack of evidence and previous statements made by known criminals that bare no weight in the court of law, with the motive behind the tainted statements". James Petrascu said. The high profile lawyer La Vieja retained, with black hair, clean shaven face, gray colored eyes, tan skin from the Miami sun he enjoys at his ten thousand square foot Villa with a resort style pool in his back yard, where he entertains his women and rich clients. " Does the government object to this?" Judge Smeltzer asked the federal prosecutor. "Yes your honor. This woman is a drug trafficker and a murderer". The female prosecutor said, looking over at the table where La Vieja and her attorneys are. " Objection your honor, this is slander, considering there's no evidence to prove her claims". Mr. Petrascu said.

"Ms. Price state the facts of your objection only". The judge said speaking to the prosecutor. She looked over at her colleague then over to the defense table, wanting La Vieja to pay for what she believes she's done to Agent Tucker and his family, along with the witnesses on this case. She wanted her to pay for the distribution of cocaine into America, flooding the east coast. Right now, she can't. The law and circumstances is on La Vieja's side. " I don't have anything further your honor ". Prosecutor Price said, seeming to lower her head with this temporary defeat. " From a legal standpoint, the U. S. Government has an obligation to uphold the law from both aspects of it. So Ms. Santiago your case is dismissed without prejudice". Judge Smeltzer said, having to honor the law he rightfully stands by. "That's bull shit!" A loud voice boomed from the back of the courtroom. All eyes shifting fast towards the disruptive voice. It's federal Agent

Tristan Thompson. "Order in the court! There will be no outburst in my court, no matter what side of the law you're on!" Judge Smeltzer stated firmly. Agent Thompson didn't respond, he only stared intently at La Vieja, as he walked out of the courtroom. La Vieja's security goons, locking his face in, in case they cross paths again. All of her security having licenses to carry weapons, under the security company she created for this sole purpose, to protect her best interest, herself. Agent Tristan Thompson a biracial male, having a black mother and white father. He stands five foot nine inches, thick muscular built, pronounced jaw line, brown eyes, that seem to be dark with his anger brewing over his good friend being killed with no justice being served. He was even invited over to Brian's house a few times for dinner. He also worked the case briefly with Agent Tucker before taking on another case that needed his immediate attention. A case he closed yesterday. When La Vieja and her goons exited the courthouse, only to be greeted by a slew of reporters, bloggers and bystanders, all wanting answers to what just took place along with her rumored connection to the cartel style massacres of the witnesses, the investigating agent and his family. "Ms. Santiago did you kill all of those attached to your case?" La Vieja ignoring the reporter. "Ms. Santiago, are you responsible for the influx in distribution of the east coast?" "Ms. Santiago are you the monster everyone is painting you out to be?" The reporters tossed back to back questions, each of them wanting their question answered. She paused in her tracks, to respond briefly. "I am not a murderer or a drug dealer, as you may think, stereotyping me and other Latinos. I'm a very successful and respected businesswoman here in Miami". She responded with a professional smile back with the confidence of being in power and control of her own destiny. " You're a fucking liar and a murderer! That's who you are!" Agent Thompson's voice boomed through the air, shifting the attention of her security, the reporters, cell phone cameras all zoomed in on him. Agent Tucker allowing his anger to cloud his vision and common sense, he removed he side arm, preparing to take aim on La Vieja, killing her for what she did to his friend and family. Without hesitation and trained precision, her goons stood in front of her, removing their weapons. Other federal agents around, rushing in on their fellow agent, stopping him. "Hey Thompson, not like this brother. We'll get this bitch, but not this way, okay?" Agent Marshall said bringing Tristan back to the reality of his job and all of the cameras rolling. La Vieja veering through her security staring Agent Thompson down as he holstered his weapon. The look in her eyes, wanting to kill him and all he loves, making him watch each of his loved ones die. Agent Thompson on the other hand, is thinking how about sleepless nights, to take her and all she values down. He want stop until she's in a set of his steel handcuffs, being aggressively stuffed into the back of his car, hauling her off to a cold concrete and steel jail cell for a sentence of Life behind bars, where she would suffer each day, knowing he put her there. She turned heading to her four vehicle convoy, jumping inside the truck. Her convoy pulling off allowing all of the bloggers, reporters to film them driving off as they filled in their own narrative to this story of a female cartel boss. Video footage from the cell phones being shared with the caption: THE FEMALE DON OF THE CARTEL. This caption, news coverage and video footage, all became a slap in the federal government's face, reminding them of the 90s when John Gotti got off so many times, he was dubbed 'The Teflon Don' . La Vieja didn't care about titles or captions. She valued respect, money and power only. Anyone in the way of this, will meet a violent demise, at the same time jeopardizing all they love.

Chapter 11

A week later Little Ki Ki slid back down Atlanta over to Karin's house in the middle of the night, making her way in around 1:46 AM. Karin was sleeping, Ki Ki used her key entering the two story brick home, boasting eighteen hundred square feet, hard wood floors throughout, two full bathrooms, one half bath in the basement. Little Ki Ki having originally fled Atlanta fearing the feds was on to her, she just up and left without even staying in contact with Karin the entire time, until now. She's missing Karin, having been away from her for six weeks. She made her way into the kitchen over to a bottle of Hennessey that's on the counter. She poured herself a double shot, downing it, then another, taking it upstairs, still undetected. The alcohol streaming through her body, taking the edge off all she's been going by through, at the same time hoping Karin welcomes her, with this absence. She came up to the open bedroom, seeing Karin sleeping peacefully. She stood in the doorway of the bedroom, to take it all in, as her suppressed emotions for this woman started coming back alive. Emotions of love she couldn't wear on her sleeve in this fast pace business. She had to put it all to the side while she focused on her new life and position up north, taking the city over. All of these things that took place also shifting her original plans to bow out of this game, so her and Karin can focus on real estate and other business ventures. Now this new position of power has her making money even when she's sleep or not around. It's far more alluring than being a block nigga breaking half a bricks down to nicks dimes and twenties. Less risk, with little to no exposure. Little Ki Ki really loves Karin equally to the loves she gets back from her. This is also why Karin patiently awaited Little Ki Ki's return, Karin knows Ki Ki's heart and how she thinks. She didn't seek another women's or man in her six week absence. She did worry, however knew she would return.

The love she instilled into her heart, made her feel that level of emotional gravitational pull, that brought her back home, where the heart is. Little Ki Ki came up on the bed, drowning the double shot, before taking hold of the red satin sheet, pulling it off of Karin's sleeping nude body, revealing the art of her beautiful body as she laying partially on her belly and side, legs parted displaying a paradise Little Ki Ki yearned for. Little Ki Ki removing her Atlanta Braves baseball cap, then her T-shirt, black jeans, followed by the sports bra and boxer briefs. One would never know with the baggie clothing, Little Ki Ki's body, youthful and picturesque with natural and perky 34c breast, flat stomach, a small waist line, that flows down to the curves of her ass and thick thighs, even her close shaven place of desire, adding to the image of her feminine art. She crawled across the bed, placing kisses up Karin's inner thighs up to her soft ass, before introducing her fingers and tongue into Karin's body. Her body although asleep, it's reacting just as her breathing, thinking she's having the best dream ever, until the sensation stirred with intensity forcing her eyes open, she looked over her shoulder gasping a heated breath, seeing it's her girl. Right then, she gave into her touch, tongue that's thrusting in and out of her warm wet body, strategically caressing and circling her clitoral pearl, creating a powerful orgasmic sensation, that's making her gyrate her hips, backing into Ki Ki's tongue and fingers. "Mmmmh, mmmmh, I love you babe, mmmmh mmmh, ooooh I miss your touch". She let out not having her touch in six weeks. This neglected body has been saved for this touch right here. Now it's ready to be released, she can't hold it back, in fact she don't want to hold it back. It's feeling so good, she want it to flow out of her. " Oooh babe, oooh babe, ooooh, ooooh, it feels so good ooooh". She moaned as the orgasmic rush, raced through her.

She moans with intensity leaving her body, her stomach clenching as Little Ki Ki isolates her pearl with her finger tips, accompanied with the speed of her tongue. "Oooh, ooooh, oooh baby, baby, baby, mmmmh, mmmmh, oooh baby". Her moans permeating through the air, as Little Ki Ki slipped her finger into Karin's ass hole, adding more sensational pressure, forcing waves of orgasms through her body, making Karin squirm, sliding over the satin sheets, off of the bed onto the floor, halting their intense sex session, at the same time they both started laughing, as Little Ki Ki, also slid off of the bed coming to Karin's side. " I love you Karin, you know me not being around was needed to protect myself as well as you, in not knowing where I was, ya feel me love?" Little Ki Ki said. "I love you too. I understand what was going on. Even if I missed you and cried myself asleep in your absence. My heart told me you would be back". Karin said, kissing her lips, feeling the affection. " This should be even more of a reason we take the money, so we can be all in on these real estate investments, getting all of the way out of the game". Karin added. Little Ki Ki looking on at her woman, her eyes luring her in, along with what she just said. Simultaneously feeling like she's caught in between this new position of power, and this woman she genuinely loves. "I want you in my life. I even want all that we plan". "Don't say but, it negates what you're saying with something you know what's right for us". Karin said cutting her off. This made Little Ki Ki reset her approach. "You want to be close to me. You can come up north when I go back. We'll buy property there away from the city life". " Does this mean you're done with the street life?" Karin asked wanting to take control of this relationship, along with their financial destiny. Little Ki Ki smiling, thinking to herself from a technical stand-point, she doesn't have to deal with the streets anymore, she's a boss.

"Yeah, no more streets. Just you and me, getting this real-estate money". Little Ki Ki responded, telling a strategic lie with partial truth. This new position of power is just as alluring as Karin's love and good sex. It makes her feel on top of the world. Plus the corrupt city of Harrisburg shows her love, being receptive to her boss bitch ways, knowing she about whatever. "Whenever you're ready, you can take me up north with you, to show me what you have in mind for investments". Karin said, always wanting to know what she's getting into, and how she can add or take away from it to make out better. "I got you shawty, right now, we going to focus back to this good thing we was having fun with until you slid off of the bed". Little Ki Ki said. Karin's fingers finding Little Ki Ki, making her let out a heated breath. " Aaah, aaaah, damn shawty, aaaah, aaaah, aaaah, right there Babycakes, aaaah, aaah, aaah, damn, you got me babe, aaaah, aaaah". Ki Ki moaned feeling her body come alive, physically and emotionally as Karin tookover, with her fingers, lips and tongue, finding Ki Ki's spot each time, allowing her feminine side to be fully exposed, as vibrant moans, heated breaths, expelled into the air, the more her orgasmic waves surged through her insides, wanting to be set free, bouncing around inside like butterflies in her belly, making her stomach clenching, tightening, trying to embrace this intense erotic sensations. She's now physically and emotionally opened as the orgasms are escaping her body. She can't hold back the pulsating sensations that surging through her body, racing over Karin's tongue and fingers. "Aaaah, aaahah, oh my God, oh my God, aaaah, aaaah, aaaah, you got me, you got me babe". Her body taken over by Karin's tongue and touch, legs shaking as orgasms escaped. This open intimate exposed side of Ki Ki will never be seen by those in the streets. They'll only witness a Atlanta female gangsta who is always in business beast mode.

Chapter 12

To celebrate evading crime and punishment from the federal government, La Vieja invited TK , Suga Baby and Red Rain, down to Miami to party on a two hundred foot super yacht, boasting luxury suites throughout, swimming pool, jacuzzi, gym, pool table, stocked bars on each level. "This is like Jay-Z's Big Pimpin video". Suga Baby said, having seen the rap legend's classic summer vibe video online. "TK I'm glad you and your lady companions could make it. Everything you see is all for you to show my appreciation, for following through on your end". La Vieja said. "The credit cannot be all mine to take. My two beautiful yet deadly ladies here, made it all possible". TK responded, directing the compliment to them. La Vieja looking over at Red Rain and Suga Baby, breaking a smile that most wouldn't see in the business, unless it was the last thing they seen from her. " It's good to see women taking care of things, displaying violence, power and drive". La Vieja said, sending a compliment their way. "Thank you. We appreciate all you do for us too, getting my girl Rain here out of that Latin King bind". Suga Baby responded, caressing Red Rain's back affectionately. La Vieja also picking up on the two looking like a couple as well as an addition to TK's life. She was impressed that this dynamic even worked out, considering the business and lifestyle of one vying for all or none of the attention and power. The staff brought champagne to everyone as they took a tour of the yacht, taking in the sumptuous amenities it has. The staff catering to them along the way, making sure their glasses stayed filled. After the tour they were seated for dinner, followed by drinks, laughter and conversation. All while coasting fifty miles off the Florida coastline. " La Vieja, you have it all with this mega yacht, money and power. I hope to one day have something like this, between the three of us as a family". Red Rain said, seeing a future of promise. "Yeah in could live on this big ass yacht, traveling the world with the two people I love". Suga Baby added. La Vieja sipping her champagne listening to how excited and inspired these two go gettas are. It reminds her of how hungry and driven she was at their age, seeking the power of her position. "TK you have two handfuls with these ladies, which is a good thing, with their vision and ambition. One day these ladies will have all they desire, including the money and power. I'll be dead, in jail, or running back to Mexico, when that day comes". La Vieja said, making the ladies know she's the boss bitch until her reign is over. Then and only then, they can have this yacht life, her power and position. " We think ahead, therefore jail or being killed off is not an option or a thing we won't see coming". Suga Baby said, repeating what her, TK and Red Rain always say to one another, to keep each other on point. "What's your endgame if you don't mind me asking?" TK asked, seeing that she does have it all financially, along with the power that comes with her position. Even the direct connect to the cartel. "Hermano, when you're in the business at this this level. You don't choose to step down or transition to the next phase. You're taken from your life, power and position, by way of death or prison. If you're smart, you may get old, rich and powerful enough, so when the time does come, it won't even matter". La Vieja responded, putting it all into perspective. Hearing her say this, while knowing how violent she can be, he didn't even want to bring up the fact, he was entertaining calling it quits, so he can be present in his child's life when Suga Baby brought their baby into this world. He also wanted to remove her from this life style to focus on being a mother, no more illegal shit that would get her caught up and taken in for that homicide beef up north. La Vieja is looking on at Suga Baby seeing that she's hasn't indulged into the alcohol, only lemon water.

She also noticed this pregnant glow she has that's undeniable. "How far along are you mami?" La Vieja asked. The question catching Suga Baby off guard. She looked at TK checking to see if he had told her. "You have that radiant glow nena". She added. " I'm three and a half months. I can't wait to bring this baby into this world". She responded, lighting up inside and out. "La familia is everything. You have to protect them with your life and love". La Vieja said. " Do you have kids?" Red Rain asked La Vieja. A question she normally wouldn't entertain. She didn't mention family to too many people, it could be deadly if the wrong people were aware of her having kids. She views TK and his lady friends as family, bonded by the blood of those they killed. "I have two teenagers, a seventeen and eighteen year old boys, who will one day have the choice of running this drug trade or the legal businesses I have". " Keeping your legacy and hard work alive huh?" Suga Baby stated. Before La Vieja was able to respond, one of her security goons came up together whispering in her ear. Her mood shift, placing everyone at the table in a different space feeling that vibe of some thing is wrong. "Excuse me, there is some business that needs my immediate attention. Continue on enjoying yourselves, you earned it". She said leaving the dining table heading to the upper deck, taking the call outside away from the others. She was told the CBP: Customs Board Patrol Agent she has on her payroll, has ran into a problem. This is not good for him, whoever or whatever the problem is. " Que pasol?" She asked what's wrong. Speaking to the agent over the phone. "There's a FBI agent here looking into all goods shipped from other countries, coming to your businesses. The agent leading this investigation name is Tristan Thompson. He seems really irate and determined to find something". The CBP agent said. This sent a burning fire through La Vieja knowing this is the same agent from the courthouse with the loud outburst. La Vieja is now on high alert, angered by this with having six tons coming in from Mexico. Three of the tons she paid cash for, the others were sent on consignment. Enough product to flood the east coast, lowering the number while supplying high quality cocaine. "Do what you need to do, to defer the container so it doesn't get searched. Make it vanish, we'll find it later". She said ending the call. What she meant by make it vanish, is to go into the computer changing the location and logging in of the containers shipped to her, especially the one with the product. If Agent Thompson found this, she wouldn't be able to get out of that, with the companies all being listed in her name, making her a Miami business elite. La Vieja, now wanting to get close and personal to Agent Thompson, to show him who he's really fucking with. This time around, she isn't planning to use TK or his deadly lady friends. She's coming with cartel power to get her respect, along with a better understanding of who's position is more powerful.

Chapter 13

The next morning, the super yacht was docking when La
Vieja's security pointed out the FBI agents were taking
pictures of them as they were getting off the yacht. Agent
Thompson, after coming up empty at the ports, thanks
to La Vieja's fast thinking and inside sources at the ports.
Agent Thompson now wanting to flex his federal position, making his presence known to create pressure,
uncomfortableness, also to let her know he and a slew of
agents under his command are watching her. His goal is
to disrupt her day to day routine, with hopes of finding
that hole in her schedule that leads to drugs or any illegal
activity to put her in a jail cell. He wanted her to pay for
what he believes she had her hands in killing Agent Brian
Tucker and his family. Even if he can't prove it, he will
make her life a living hell, legally and illegally, until she's
dead or locked up behind bars for life. "Be safe and have
a watchful eye hermano. That puta is trying to stir things
up". La Vieja said to TK referring to the FBI agent. "The
FBI is taking our pictures over there. Them putas don't
know who they're fucking with, until it's too late ". She
added, angered by the FBI's presence, especially Agent
Thompson who she believes is disrespectful, deserving of
a bullet to his face. TK and the ladies looking into the

direction of the feds snapping pictures, feeling compromised. Suga Baby being on the run from PA, for murder. Her heart and mind is racing, thinking about her baby, going to jail being separated from her child. This is not good or an option She's thinking. She would rather be dead, than to have that be her end. " Hermano the new shipment will be delayed until I deal with this piece of shit". La Vieja said, knowing Agent Thompson will be around until she makes him respect her cartel gangster in a language he can understand. "I also advise you and your team to be mindful of who you bring into your circle. They'll come at all around me. I'll do what I can on my end, to make sure I cut the head off of this snake". La Vieja said. "So you know, if shit hits the fan, our loyalty is til the death. We don't do jail. We hold court in the streets". TK responded, never wanting to ever go back to jail again. La Vieja nodded before one of her cars, a Bentley Flying Spur picked TK, and the ladies up, driving them to the airport. The car drove pass the cars where the federal agents are snapping photos. Suga Baby putting up the middle finger as they drove pass. "I hate them mutha fuckas". Suga Baby said. At the same time TK was thinking about why this should be the end of his reign. He came, he saw he concurred, way more than he imagined or planned when he was up state. Is this the life I want for my unborn child? He's questioning himself. He also started reflecting back to what La Vieja said about the two ways out of this business, when you're at this level of position and power. La Vieja got into her Rolls Royce Phantom, all black, inside and out, even the tinted windows. Her security in front and behind her in other vehicles. "Senora, them cabron's is following us". Her security said, making her aware of the federal agent's presence. La Vieja's eyes became dark, just as her thoughts of what she wants to do to this piece of shit. " Pull over so I can talk to this pendejo". She said puffing her cigarette. She exited the car walking back to the lead car following them. Right then she recognized the familiar face of Agent Thompson. This fueled her anger even more, as he rolled the window down, the agent in the passenger seat took out his phone to record her in case things became violent or she said something incriminating. She blew smoke into the agent's face, really wishing she could unload a clip into his face right now. Killing him has to be different, where he isn't prepared and doesn't see it coming. "I don't play games I know I can't win, Agent Thompson. You're playing a very dangerous game you can't win". La Vieja said.

The taunting smirk on his face disappeared hearing her say this. "What? You think this is a game!? You're a murderous immigrant flooding the streets of America with cocaine, poisoning the kids and their families!" He snapped, being offended by her approach, as if she isn't the biggest criminal in Miami, if not the east coast. His response also displayed his prejudice stance in pursing her. "I'm a hard working businesswoman. Immigrant or not, my success comes from my hard labor and ambition to succeed, having all I please. Nothing else as you may think or stereotype me and those with my ethnic background". "Get the fuck out of here with the lies and bullshit! You're a fucking murdering drug dealer! I will be the one to bust your ass, slamming the cuffs on you with a smile. I'll never let up until you're in a jail cell where you belong, with the rest of the border hoppers!" He stated, displaying aggression and prejudice. She also picked up on it, staring him down, with so many murderous thoughts racing through her mind of how she wanted him to pay for his disrespect and prejudice. Her anger arising to the point a part of her is wanting to walk back to convoy, to get one of her security goon's gun, only to return with murder and malice on her mind, killing this prejudice scum bag and his partner who is sitting there recording like a teenage kid watching a fight at school. Instead her calm response set in place war between them. "Well then, let's see who's watching who the closest. I've been known to be keen on the smallest details most people tend to overlook". She stated puffing her cigarette blowing smoke into the car and his face before turning to leave him with that thought. Little did he know, she's going to be gunning for him as much as he's tracking her. The only difference, she's going to be pursuing him and all he loves, placing them in danger. She doesn't have to play by the rules of the law as he does, giving her the advantage.

Chapter 14

Two months later, the effects of Agent Thompson along with the federal agents under his command, cracking down on La Vieja. It's being felt up and down the east coast. La Vieja even had more product sent, hoping to get it through, all to no avail. She was forced to hide that shipping container too. Now with the twelve tons being hidden at the ports, the east coast is feeling it trickle all the way down to the blocks.

This angered her, not having any product to sell, yet still having to pay her cartel boss his money, because excuses doesn't pay him. The shutdown as they all know, opens up doors for rival cartels to move in on her established territory.

As for TK, his team offed the last of the product they had too. This left Little Ki Ki supplying the north with what she had left. She left it all raw, not cutting it or raising the prices, still staying competitive. Amidst the chaos with the Agent Thompson, La Vieja set in place her next move. Agent Thompson was leaving work after a long day set out to bust La Vieja for something. He jumped into his car, talking on his phone, unaware of the tail on him. He was so focused on talking to his pregnant wife who is now seven moths along.

"Hey honey, I'll be home a little late, I'm still working this case". Agent Thompson said.

"I'll have a plate made for you in the fridge. Be safe and make it home to us". She responded.

"I will. I love you honey".

"I love you too". She said meaning every word, honoring her husband to the fullest. He on the other hand, hung up the phone with his mistress on his mind. A lady of the night he wanted to keep seeing over and over. He found her on-line, having been intimate with her for the last few months, instead of loving his wife as she does him. He found this young exotic blond with a golden tan, that would do things to him and for him, his wife wouldn't dare do or think of. While he's driving to the reserved room at the Holiday Inn, he's being followed by La Vieja's cartel goons, keeping close tabs on him as they've been, since he made his presence known at the pier when she was departing her yacht. Agent Thompson now making it to his room, having a key card coming into see his blond mistress in a powder blue lingerie, with drink in her hand, adult toys on the night stand, setting the mood. His level of excitement is high, undressing, coming over to her kissing her lips, then her neck, before pausing to get a drink of the EJ Brandy.

Outside of the hotel room, La Vieja's goons were getting in place as strategically planned to wait long enough until he's fully exposed and vulnerable. They waited for thirty minutes to pass by.

Then It happened.

The hotel door was breach fast with force as Miami Dade Police officers stormed the room. All of these men on La Vieja's payroll. Tristan was face deep in between the blond's legs giving her oral pleasure. He jumped up quick with his face and lips glistening from her fluids.

"What the hell is this!?" Tristan snapped feeling compromised on many levels. "I'm a federal agent!" He blurted out, as if to help his situation.

"We've been monitoring this hotel for human trafficking, prostitution and other illegal activities. That young lady we've seen her around, she's a lady of the night". The officer said looking at the young lady then back to Agent Thompson.

"She looks kind of young too sir". Another officer chimed in. "Do you have any ID young lady?" He continued. The female obliged grabbing her ID off of the nightstand, handing it to the officer. At the same time, Agent Thompson is feeling embarrassed and compromised, not knowing how he would be able to explain this to his pregnant wife or he superiors at the bureau. "This ID is fake! We're going to have to haul her in too, for falsified documents, unless you tell us your real name and age". The officer said, sending fear into her and Agent Thompson knowing if her ID is fake, so is her name and age she told him.

"My real name is Melanie Markel, I'm fifteen, it's not his fault". She responded, knowing she deceived him, with the fake ID, looking more like twenty one as she made him believe.

"Bitch! You lied to me! This is statutory rape!" Agent Tucker snapped realizing on top of prostitution, cheating on his wife, he'll be facing a rape beef too. This is not good at all, he can't explain his way out of this.

"Sir you're under arrest for prostitution, trafficking of a minor, and statutory rape. Can you get dress and turn around". One of the five Miami Dade Police officers said. Each of them having their guns out in hand in case he tried to be foolish in resisting this arrest to evade the inevitable.

"Can I call my wife?"

"You'll have that chance once you're booked in at the station". The officer replied. The officers, also securing the female that is also the victim in this matter. They took pictures and video footage of them on the bed together. They also have evidence of this room being registered in his name. They took Tristan out to the squad car, placing him in the back seat. His whole world is crashing as thoughts of how this is all going to unfold, with him losing his job, wife, and jail time.

Ten minutes later, the police car pulled into a off street, along side a convoy of Range Rover Sport trucks. The back window of the truck came down as the officers removed Tristan from the back seat of the squad car. When he seen La Vieja's face, his blood pressure spiked, coupled with anger, allowing her to outsmart him, in using his own weakness against him. The smirk on her face even tore through him, like a razor sharp knife, cutting deep, where it hurts the most.

"You set me up!" Agent Tucker snapped.

"No, I only exposed your true identity, as a cheater, a rapist and a criminal". She responded with calm, displaying control.

"I ain't no fucking rapist! This is some bull shit and you know it!" He responded, angered knowing a charge like this in prison will make him a target, by real criminals, that despise rapist and pedophiles.

"Agent Thompson, call your dogs off at the ports right now. Then this thing you got yourself in, will go away, like it never happened, until you forget who is in charge". La Vieja said, giving him an out, from this dark situation he found himself in. The proud agent in him is wanting to resist her proposal, now knowing she does have product at the ports his team overlooked. If he says no to her, what happens next will wipe his marriage and career out totally, leaving him with nothing but a jail cell.

"Give me my phone". Agent Thompson demanded, so he can make the call. The officer who took his phone, now holding it in front of him, dialing the number to the other agents, that are combing the ports in search of the shipment.

"Tristan, we don't have anything yet. We are looking over paperwork, that says other shipments landed". Agent Marshall said.

"Hey Marshall, it's not coming in that way. I just got a solid tip from my CIs, saying, it'll be coming in by the truck loads this week. So stop wasting time over there. I'll see you all in the office in the morning". The call ended. Tristan now wanting to be released from this position of humility. "I gave you what you wanted. Now tell these idiots to uncuff me". Agent Thompson said. La Vieja giving him this look, searching for his truth, how he would respond to her compromising him like this, forcing his hand to allow her shipments in.

"You did what you had to do, because I gave you no other choice". La Vieja said, before looking over to her corrupt Miami Dade police officers. "Oye mata lo". She told them to kill him.The window rolled up. They took the cuffs off of him, giving him his gun back before, firing on the agent, killing him with a head a center mass shots. Then they fired his weapon to show discharge of him resisting arrest. This level of masterminding comes with the position of power, in order to stay alive in this game.

Chapter 15

Two weeks later, the east coast is being flooded with raw fish scale cocaine. Life for everyone that's connected to the plug, is getting money, splurging and investing. Little Ki Ki and Karin purchased a fifty five hundred square foot home in the Fox Hills Estates. Located in the suburbs of Harrisburg. The home outfitted with white marble floors, white granite counter tops in the kitchen, his and her walk in closets, large walk in glass shower with rain shower head and jet sprayers, that came out of the wall for added pleasure. Two fire places, one in the master bedroom, the other in the living room. The four large bedrooms having full baths, along with two half baths on the first floor and the lower entertainment level. The home also boasting a three car garage, where Karin keeps her Infinity QX60 truck, along with her midnight blue BMW XI Electric truck. Little Ki Ki, had her four wheeler, a all black 900 Ninja, inside of the garage. She also pushed a low key gray Honda Accord, not being flashy. Her only splurge is her new crib, plus the three carat diamond engagement ring she gave Karin, expressing her love and desire to spend the rest of her days being true to her. Little Ki Ki using her intelligence and position, she put Bundles in charge of the city moving product to everyone in the hood.

Little Ki Ki made sure Trappa-D and his young bucks had paid lawyers, money on their books and whatever they needed. She established contact once she seen that he took all of the beef, clearing her of any connection to the hood in ATL. For his loyalty, he nor his family will never want for anything. She also told him to plea out when it comes to the feds, knowing they will roof him if he went to trial. If he pleas out, his cap could be 120 months to 240 months. Either way his time will be as comfortable as money could make it, as long as Little Ki Ki is in position. While Little Ki Ki is in her living room enjoying her best life on top, in a position of power. Down south in Atlanta, Suga Baby is now six months pregnant, belly showing. This didn't stop her wanting to look sexy, while showing off her baby bump. Her and Red Rain is out baby clothes shopping, at the same time positing pictures on Instagram, for Red Rain's fan base, that has a million plus Followers. All due to her lady boss life style, and sexy curves, giving her Followers a intimate look inside her life, even sexy time, before it gets heated, then she cuts them off. Little Ki Ki hit Red Rain up on her cell phone, wanting to holla at her about a few things, to keep them on point.

"What it do shawty? How's the north treating you?" Red Rain asked answering her phone, having Little Ki Ki on face time.

"It's a lot of love up here ya feel me?" She responded showing Red Rain Karin's hand with the diamond engagement on it.

"Congratulations shawty you booing it up huh? We better be bridesmaids". Red Rain responded. Suga Baby rubbing her belly as Red Rain is showing her off to Little Ki Ki.

"Look at you lil mamma, with that life growing inside of ya". Little Ki Ki said smiling.

"Yeah I can't wait to have this baby. You see we out here shopping to spoil my baby boy when he gets here". Suga Baby said, full of excitement ready to be a mom.

"Oh you having a little TK that's going take over shit huh?"

"A little bad ass". Red Rain added.

"He's going to be a momma's boy, not a bad ass". Suga Baby said defending her baby boy.

"Say shawty, tone it down on the gram with Suga Baby in the view, ya feel me? She still dodging them folks, so you can't shine the light with a million plus tuned in, ya hear me?" Ki Ki said pulling Red Rain up on this, at the same time, it brought life and everything else into perspective to Suga Baby, especially with that fact, being pushed to the back of her mind, having been on the run for so long, also being at the top of her game in this business.

"Good looking baby girl, we love you down her in the A, in case you and Karin get homesick, don't forget where y'all came from". Red Rain said. They all laughed before hanging up the phone. Red Rain continued to snap selfies, along with buying baby clothing for her Godson. Suga Baby was tuned in, noticing this white male with a baseball cap and shades on, looking like he's watching them.

"Let's go, I think we have enough". Suga Baby said getting this bad feeling. Her hood instincts is kicking in, alerting her. Red Rain picking up on her sudden mood change.

"Is this pregnancy wearing you out babe?" Red Rain asked stepping closer kissing her cheek.

"Something don't feel right". She responded.

Red Rain looking down at her belly.

"Is junior okay in there?" She questioned in fear.

"It's not the baby. I think we're being watched". She responded.

Hearing her say this, made Red Rain go into protective beast mode, adjusting the handbag with her Glock inside.

"Let's go check out, unless you want to leave this shit and I'll come back for it?"

"Leave it". Suga Baby said, seeing man in the ball cap looking like he's communicating with someone else. Not good! She's thinking and feeling, having this child inside of her. Jail isn't a place for a pregnant woman to be at. They headed towards the exit, Suga Baby is holding her belly for comfort with one hand. The other hand inside of her handbag, holding onto the 9mm Sig Sauer, safety off, one in the chamber, sixteen in the clip. As she was walking through the automatic sliding doors, there's another man outside of the store, with his eyes locked on them. Is it the feds? Local drug task force or homicide? So many thoughts, none of which she wanted to stick around to confirm.

"Keisha Jackson!" A male voice called out from behind them. Both Suga Baby and Red Rain ignoring her real name being called out. A level of intense fear and adrenaline, spiking in both of them as they continued walking towards the charcoal grey Maseratti with burgundy interior.

The male came up behind them, placing his hand on Suga Baby's shoulder. Her mind went into overdrive, thinking about protecting herself and baby, by any means necessary.

"Keisha Jackson!" The male called out again. Everything slowed down, as she turned looking over her shoulder, seeing the visible badge dangling. She didn't care, her finger inside of the trigger guard, squeezing the trigger, firing back to back rounds through the handbag hanging off of her shoulder. Slugs slamming into the officer. His body thrusting back, forcing him off of his feet. At the same time Red Rain removed her Glock 40mm aiming it at the fast approaching man that seem to be with the officer, especially with his gun out. She fired on him multiple times forcing him to take cover.

"Get in the car!" Red Rain yelled out to Suga Baby as she scanned the area for more undercover officers. No one else, just these two; Detective Wilson and his new partner William Packard, from Harrisburg. Red Rain jumped into the Maseratti, starting it up, backing out before mashing the gas. Detective Wilson running and gunning, sending over a dozen slugs through the air into the back of the Maseratti window and trunk, making Red Rain swerve mashing the gas to accelerate to evade being hit.

"I'm hit bitch!" Suga Baby said feeling the burning sensation of the hot moulting slugs, that went through the trunk into her back.

"I should have put a bullet in his fucking face!" Red Rain snapped, before adding. "I'm a get you to a hospital, don't worry baby, I got you".

"No, no, I'll go to jail, they'll take my baby". She responded still trying to protect her baby.

"Call TK". Red Rain said hitting the phone button on the steering wheel.

"What's good?" He answered on the second ring.

"Keisha got shot by the cops. She don't want to go to the hospital". Red Rain said, with evident fear in her voice, caring about her girl's well being.

"Bring her home, I'll make a few calls to make sure she's good". He replied.

As she was driving, merging onto the highway to the house, she can see flashing lights and fast driving police cars heading towards the plaza they were just at. The social media postings drew Detective Wilson to Atlanta, having one of his CIs put him onto the exotic yet deadly Red Rain. So he started Following her under a anonymous name, watching each time she showed Suga Baby, which allowed him to know how close they are. So he and his new partner attempted to confront Suga Baby, even with her being pregnant having the baby weight and new hair color and style, she still has a unforgettable face. Back at the house TK made calls around to a few people he met being in the Atlanta circle of powerful black elites, from lawyers, doctors to politicians. All people he can count on, as well as people that look forward to his generous donations when the time comes.

Back inside of the car Red Rain is driving fast rubbing Suga Baby's belly, trying to comfort her and her Godson inside.

"You're going to be okay babe, you and my Godson".

"I don't feel like it. Something is wrong Rain, he was moving around wild, then he stopped". Suga Baby said in fear of losing her child. She wanted him to be safe, even if she was to bleed out.

"Don't trip babe the baby is good, it's just the excitement and your adrenaline. Now stay calm, because he can feel your emotions and stress, okay babe. I love you. You're going to be good". Red Rain said still caressing her belly, doing over a hundred on the highway, checking the rearview mirror, making sure no one is chasing behind them on their way to their new seven thousand square foot house, with all of the lavish amenities to appease a east coast boss and his two ride or die queens.

Chapter 16

Red Rain is driving fast down the street where they live, seeing Suga Baby is going in and out. All due to physical stress and trauma.

"We're home baby, everything is going to be okay". Red Rain said pulling into the driveway. TK waiving her into the garage, where Doctor Elijah Kiptinue and his two registered nurse assistance are. She pulled in closing the garage door behind them. The doctor already having a makeshift set up, inside the garage, with all of his needed medical supplies to expedite these emergency medical procedures. Especially having heard the person he's going to be tending to is pregnant. Dr. Kiptinue being a Nigerian born man, standing six foot one, dark radiant skin tone, hair cut close, perfect white teeth when he smiles to comfort his patients. Still having the African accent, giving those in his presence the sounds of the motherland. They helped Suga Baby from the car. Her eyes closed having went out again. They placed her on the cushioned table as the nurses and doctor worked their medical magic. Red Rain holding on to TK in tears, fearing losing Suga Baby or her Godson inside of her. TK stood having the same thoughts, back by killing the cops responsible for this, after he makes them suffer, feeling the pain he's enduring emotionally right now at the thought of this woman he loves slipping away from him with their child too. The doctor continued tending to her wounds as the nurses checked on the wellbeing of the baby, using a portable sonogram machine, in search of the baby's heart beat.

"Oh there you are". The nurse said finding the baby's heart beat.

"Rough day, but you're a survivor huh?" She added seeing the images of the baby that's untouched from the bullets that entered his mother's body. With the amount of stress of the situation, the level of adrenaline surging through her, accompanied with the trauma of being shot, the baby was wound up, exerting itself before going to sleep, which made Suga Baby think something was wrong with the baby. These thoughts along with the same trauma also made her black out. "Is the baby going to be okay?" Red Rain questioned with a broken emotional tone of voice.

"Yes, he's a strong little fella". The nurse responded.

"What about her, she good?" TK asked, feeling that crushing weight lifted off his body, knowing his son will make it.

"I removed two slugs from the back muscle. Had it went a inch deeper or to the left or right, we would be saving the baby's life and not hers. She'll be fine after a little rest". Dr. Kiptinue said before adding.

"I'll leave one of my assistance here to look after her medical needs, meds, and bandages. If anything comes up with her or the baby, she'll be here to help then alert me".

He was referring to the Somalian born female standing five foot ten, slim built with a beautiful dimples in her warm smile. Long brown hair, brown eyes that seem to say hello, or it's okay. Sabrina Shabazz is her name. TK had given the doctor a hundred grand for this random house call, which includes the service of Sabrina.

"Good looking doc, you already know anything I can do for you or your team just asked". TK said being appreciative of him saving Suga Baby and his son. After shaking the doctor's hand, he and his other assistant left, leaving TK, Red Rain and to carry Suga Baby into the first floor master suite. TK and Red Rain stepped out of the room to discuss what's next for them.

"When she's able to travel. I need you to take her out of the country. Anywhere safe, so she can have the baby without the stress all this game brings, including the cops that's looking for her". TK said. Red Rain loving both Suga Baby and TK, she didn't want to be apart from neither of them, however she knew this is for he best for the future of their family.

"I'll do anything for my bitch and god son. What about the business and our positions?"

"It'll run smooth with Little Ki Ki holding it down expanding up north and out the Midwest. I'll secure down here. Maybe even find some real niggas that's about that life, so I can step away and collect this paper while I'm in the country you and Keisha land in". TK said. He also want Red Rain and Suga Baby out of the way, while he makes the cop pay for the mistake of harming what he loves.

"I'll do whatever it takes to protect her, our love, family and empire". Red Rain said.

TK pulling her close for comfort, missing her forehead, then her soft lips. Each of them having this level of love and inseparable bond. They parted from the kiss, making their way back into the bedroom. Red Rain climbing up on the bed, laying beside Suga Baby, caressing her belly affectionately. TK came over, kissing her cheek. Her eyes opening, feeling his presence and affection.

"Is my baby okay? " Suga Baby questioned, feeling Red Rain's hand on her belly.

"He's a survivor like his dad". Red Rain responded, looking up at TK seeing if he's going to break it to her about leaving the country.

"Keisha, I love you, Shandrea and junior inside of you, more than words can explain. I would do anything for all of y'all. This means protecting you too".

"Just tell me you don't want me in this game anymore". Suga Baby said thinking that was the totality of his thoughts.

"You and Shandrea are leaving the country for awhile, so you can have the baby in comfort. You can't be here in the States right now, it's hot and too risky. Especially Atlanta, this city is compromised ground for you". TK stated.

"I don't want to leave you babe". She pleaded being emotional. He wiped her tears.

"I'll be right behind y'all, once you get situated. This is about you and our son being safe, free and in comfort without looking over your shoulders ". TK responded.

"I'm tired, let me think about it". She said closing her eyes not wanting to deal with it right now. Her eyes open or closed, TK has his mind made up to protect what he loves in both of these women and his child.

Chapter 17

4:47 AM TK, Suga Baby, Red Rain and Nurse Sabrina are all asleep, after a long exhausting day, that was overbearing with stress, emotions and physical pain. All taking its toll on them, forcing them into a heavy sleep, until a chiming sound from the motion detectors around the house exterior sounded off. Sabrina awoke first being a nurse, thinking it was a monitor going off. She looked over at the sixty inch screen mounted on the wall that turned on in synch to the motion detector going off. Sabrina can see multiple bodies moving around on each screen. Men carrying weapons, looking to be SWAT or a local tactical team.

Her heart started beating fast. Her mind going into overdrive to save her patient slash client. She shook TK awake displaying her urgency. He leaped from his sleep, pulling away from Sabrina's grip shaking him. Her eyes wide pointing at the TV screen.

"Something is wrong". She said. When he turned to see the screen, the men moving around. A powerful dose of adrenaline spiked through is body forcing him into protective mode, waking up Red Rain and Suga Baby. He held his index finger to this mouth for them to move in silence. Sabrina helped Suga Baby up.

"I got it from here ". Red Rain said, taking Suga Baby with her into the large walk in closet. Thinking safe and ahead to protect Suga Baby with her life.

"Sabrina, get rid of that medical shit, then toss them scrubs into the laundry. Put some of their pajamas on". TK said looking up at the monitor, seeing his house is surrounded by Atlanta Police. After the shootout earlier today, Detective Wilson had all of the cameras in the stores with angles of the shooting, reviewed, tracking the registration of the car that lead them to this address. The Maseratti in Red Rain's name lead them here. Now her and Suga Baby are wanted for attempted homicide on a police officer along with Suga Baby's Pennsylvania's homicide warrant. TK made his way to the front door, removing his cell phone, calling in a favor from Tiffany Dupri, the Mayor of Atlanta. A respected figure with connections in the political arena. She's also someone he donated over a half of million to, for strategic purposes, like now. As the phone started ringing, he opened the door to the police officers looking shocked by his presence, when they thought they had the element of surprise.

"This better be important, waking me up at four in the morning". Mayor Dupri said.

"I called you, seeing there's a dozen police officers setting off my motion sensors".

"Atlanta PD we have two body warrants for Keisha Jackson and Shandrea Richards". The officer said, formally announcing himself and cause for legal purposes.

"They ain't here". TK responded, still standing in the door way, blocking their entrance, stalling.

"What is it you need me to do, if they have legitimate warrants?" Mayor Dupri questioned. TK put the phone on speaker.

"I called you Mayor Dupri, to make sure your officers respect me and my property, as they would the rest of the respected tax payers in this city". TK said.

"Who's the lead officer?" She asked.

"I am ma'am. It's me Sergeant Grove". The officer at the door announced.

"Look for who you all came for, anything else won't stand in the court of law ". She said.

"Yes ma'am ".

"Take me off speaker". She demanded. He did just that, also respecting her political position of power.

"I'm here". TK said making her aware that he took her off speaker.

"Don't say or do anything that will incriminate your-self. They came for your pretty lady friends. I will not ask why. The less I know the better. I hope they're not there, no matter what they did. Now let me get back to sleep, I have a meeting at nine". She said hanging up.

The detectives and Atlanta PD toned down their original approach, since they were coming with surprise, brute force, and gunfire, having two officers of the law fired on by these deadly women. The dozen or so officers combed through the large home, coming across the female laying on the bed in short pajamas shorts with a matching bra. No sign of Suga Baby or Red Rain. The officers came into the attached garage, immediately seeing the car that was involved in the cop shooting.

"Sir, this is the car! Look at all of the bullet holes". One of the officers said to Sergeant Grove, getting this rush pumped up having discovered this, which is making them think their suspects are here or was here.

"Detective Wilson, come in here!" Sergeant Grove yelled out. Detective Wilson and his partner came in the garage, seeing the car, briefly flashing back to the shoot out. The detectives raced back out to where TK stood in the foyer, waiting on these clowns to get the fuck out of his crib.

"Where the hell are they!? That's the fucking car she was driving! I should have put a bullet in that bitches head!" Detective Wilson snapped. TK staring back at him, holding his tongue, now knowing this is the one responsible for shooting at the women he loves, bringing harm to one of them, while endangering the life of his unborn son.

"Like I said they not here".

"That's her god damn car!" Detective Wilson fired back, then added. "We're taking that car for evidence. You better be glad she's not here!" He rambled on emotionally venting, having been shot at.

"Get what you came for, then excuse yourself while you can". TK said eyeing Detective Wilson, wanting to put a bullet in his face right here, right now, for shooting Suga Baby.

"What!?" He snapped turning back to TK, until other officers and his partner took hold of him, directing him out of the house, while they called for the tow truck. The other officers having spent a hour in the large home searching every inch, or so they thought. This home is outfitted with a safe room, that is sound proof, bomb proof, fire proof, with dry and canned goods to last two months if need be. This safe room isn't on the home's original plans. It was custom built by the first home owner, who moved to a larger home, once they secured a new contract in the football league out west. TK nor the ladies thought they would ever have to use it, especially Suga Baby, who always thought she would die in a gun fight, when the cops put her back against the wall. This room became a blessing in disguise, protecting her and her unborn child.

5:17AM The police are all gone except for Detective Wilson and his partner. Both of them are in the rental car, parked across from TK's large home. He's just sitting there staring back up at the house. TK can see him on the sixty inch TV monitor. Sabrina pointed that out to him. He was trippen on how driven this cop is, even after he came up empty handed.

"Good looking Sabrina. You can get dressed now". TK said, seeing she's wearing Suga Baby's pajamas shorts. It looks good on her, but that's not where his mind or heart is at right now. He has two of the baddest bitches that he has his way with. Going outside of that would be a death wish and the demise of this emotional, mental and physical pact they have.

TK waited for Sabrina to get out of Suga Baby's cloth-ing before getting them out. Sabrina wasn't aware of the safe room on the other side of the walk in closet. She just figured the cops overlooked them.

"They gone?" Red Rain asked.

"Except for that mutha fucking PA detective that shot her". TK responded, then added. "Wait him out, then y'all both leave. I'll connect with you when you get to where you're going". He said, pulling them together, embracing this change in his life without the physical, mental, and emotional comfort of their presence. Now he has to focus on this business securing all that is needed to make his exit. He didn't plan on sticking around, waiting to be arrested or taken out by someone wanting his position of power. For him, he got exactly what he wanted and more.

Chapter 18

When the sun came up, Red Rain and Suga Baby left the house, heading down Miami, where La Vieja using her resources to get them on a boat to Havana, Cuba. Once they got to Cuba, they were met by some of La Vieja's associates that looked after them, taking them to a house, they felt comfortable at. TK is on his phone face timing with them, since they wanted to show him that they're safe, in this two story brick home, close to tourist attractions.

They found it funny, seeing all of the old cars and restored buildings. As for the place they're in, it's up to hotel standards, with La Vieja's associates renting it out when tourist come from other countries.

"This place isn't as bad as I envisioned it. Only thing missing now is you". Suga Baby said.

"You better be here when the baby comes, so we can bring junior into this world as a family". Red Rain added standing behind Suga Baby.

"I'll be there even if I have to swim to Cuba". TK responded.

"You can't swim babe". Suga Baby said, remembering going swimming with him and Rain at a resort they was at. He stayed on the edge, in the shallow waters.

"Yo chill, I'll still get there in a body bag". He tossed back, being funny, yet allowing them to know he would be there to see his son born, no matter what. "All right, I love y'all. I have some business that I has to be taken care of". TK said having flown to PA, soon as they left the house this morning. He wanted to run his new business plans to Little Ki Ki in person, to put her down with the changes, and increase in shipment from La Vieja minus Suga Baby and Red Rain, his main ridas.

"We love you too babe, all three of us". Red Rain said coming into view rubbing Suga Baby's belly.

"When I'm done securing shit up here, I'll be down there. Until then, both of y'all sexy beast be good". He said ending the call. TK has a stop that needs his attention before he holla at Little Ki Ki. He made his way to Detective Wilson's house located in Highland Gardens, located in Camp Hill, Pennsylvania. A town five minutes outside of Harrisburg. TK got all of this information from the many Instagram, Twitter, and Facebook post on social media. Some things aren't meant to be shared, including their home they were so excited about when they first purchased it, showing it off on-line. Never did they ever think, Detects Wilson's job would lead to this.

TK pulled into the driveway of two story brick home, in a Ford Explore rental he got at the airport. He exited looking business savvy, wearing a navy blue two piece Kenneth Cole, tailored to his fit frame. The black Shoe by Kenneth Cole also flowing with his business look. He rang the doorbell, followed by a knock on the door. No one answered as he continued to look around to make sure no one had the door cameras or outside security systems that would pick him up. From what he can see, there is nothing. TK notice a woman coming his way walking with a little boy looking no more than four or five years old. The closer she got, he also noticed, she's pregnant. She's looking at him along with her son, that's pointing at TK.

"Excuse me, can I help you?" The female asked, now within ten yards, turning into the driveway.

"Yes, I'm Mark Tate. I came to bring Donnie that classified info he wanted for a case he's working". TK said changing the cadence of his voice to sound more professional. His response, misdirection of having classified info, making himself sound and seem important to her, coupled with his well groomed good looking attire. She being naive fell right into it.

"He's not home right now, if you like you can leave it with me, along with your card in case I forget your name". She said. TK pretending to be hesitant, seeing she's now at the door fondling with the lock and key.

"One second, let me grab it out of the truck". He said going back to the truck opening the glove compartment, reaching like he's getting something. He came back over to the door that's now open. He's still smiling to send comfort, calm her way, as he reached inside of his jacket pocket, he step forward removing a switch blade he hit, flipping the shining sharp blade, placing it to her neck. A jolting level of fear, leaping through her body.

"Please! Not in front of my baby boy". She said, holding her son's hand tight as he pushed her into the house, closing the door behind them. TK could have paid anyone to do what he's about to do, but this right here is personal. When he seen Suga Baby's limp body being pulled from the car, he felt helpless, thinking he was going to lose her. Then the disrespect of Detective Wilson talking shit to him, about putting a bullet in her head. Now TK want Detective Wilson to feel his wrath and pain.

"Don't rape me, I'm pregnant, just take whatever you want". Mrs. Wilson pleaded. TK snatched her son from her, placing the knife to his throat. The little boy not understanding the magnitude of this violent position he's in, tried to push the knife away.

"Nooo! Don't hurt him!" She screamed.

"Do I look like a rapist or a mutha fucking thief?" TK snapped, now allowing her to hear his real gangsta tone of voice. "Your husband's line of work and disrespect put you in this position". TK said not hesitating to slice the little boy's throat with force, opening his neck up as he gagged for air, in immense fear. The mother froze in shock, trauma and fear, sucking in a dry painful breath. In the same motion, TK slammed the knife into her pregnant stomach, then her heart over and over venting, unleashing a murderous rage, until she stopped moving. This level of rage and adrenaline spiking through his body, forcing him to breathe heavy. He pulled himself together cleaning up any traces of his presence. Even the blood from himself, before he exited feeling good about getting revenge on this bitch ass cop. He calmly walked back to the truck, driving off, leaving behind a crime scene of deep pain for Detective Wilson to discover.

Chapter 19

TK switched rentals, changing his clothes, showered at the Hilton, before linking up with Little Ki Ki at the Magic Wok, on Market Street, located on the Hillside of the city. The Chinese take out owned by Joel Li, who also owns Chan's Uptown. TK grabbed some chicken wings and fries. Little Ki Ki got the pork rib tips with a Coke-a-Cola. They stepped outside watching the traffic of the hood and surrounding stores, all fast pace movement of the city life. Each of them on point, at the same time, being here in the hood keeps them grounded, staying hungry like they're still on the block grinding or taking money.

"Sorry to hear about baby girl getting hit up. She good now right?" Little Ki Ki said.

"Yeah shit got crazy, it was way too close to home, so I had them leave the country for awhile. Which is why I'm here personally to holla at you". TK said. She looked over at him eating her pork rib tips, ready to hear this new change good or bad. She fucks with TK, so she'll ride with whatever he say. "I got a shipment increase coming through. You being the only one I trust on this level, with heavy content, since my ladies are on a little vacation".

"You already know I got you folk. I was expanding out Philly and Chicago. Plus I'm giving these New York niggas a run for they paper, with the numbers and quality".

"With this new thing coming through, you'll be able to hit them with even better numbers, to shut all of these mutha fuckas down". As they're talking, gunfire erupted down the street. Both of them shifting their heads to the live sounds of the hood, seeing two females popping off at this nigga on the ground.

"Yo we out before the cops come". Little Ki Ki said not wanting to be tagged as a witness. They drove to her crib in Forest Hills. TK was impressed seeing the little hommie grow in this game, spending her money wisely, not being flashy. Her only lavish expense is this home. The rest of her money is invested in real estate, Dodge and Bit Coin.

Karin put her onto this, wanting to secure their future.

"Trappa-D would trip if he seen how you living now, when he too can have the same, instead of the jewels and cars he chose". TK said, looking on at the crib walking in.

"I be looking out for him, making sure his books is right, sending him magazines, and all that jail shit. Plus when he touch, I got shit set up for him, so he wants for nothing ". Little Ki Ki said, especially having grew up with Trappa-D since they was five years old. He was like a brother to her. " My lady is out right now or I would introduce you two, ya feel me?"

"What she do?" He asked wanting to know if she was up on the life she lives.

"Real Estate", Little Ki Ki responded pointing to the crib, walking into the living room area to give TK a tour. Right then, she halted in her tracks, seeing four Latinos, guns out. Two of them having their guns pointing down, which made Little Ki Ki's eyes follow, only to see Karin bounded and gagged on the floor. Her truck must be in the garage, which is why Little Ki Ki thought she wasn't home.

TK immediately noticing and remembering the Latinos, it's Don Rico and Tito. The other two Latin Kings he never seen before.

"I don't know who y'all Spanish niggas is, but we all going die today, you hurt baby girl, ya feel me!" Little Ki Ki snapped removing the twin snub .45 Black Eagles automatics, aiming both at the two having their guns aimed at Karin.

"Espera!" Don Rico yelled out wait, to his goons. "Hermano, you are everywhere. First you send that pretty bitch to flood the city, now you have this girl boy taking over".

"Watch ya mouth fo I put slugs in it!" Little Ki Ki stated firmly, not taking to his disrespect.

"Don Rico you think because you're in a gang, you got shit on lock? You want the power I have as you've witnessed first hand, can kill anyone you love or care about". TK stated standing firm on his position of power. Don Rico didn't make the same mistake as before, leaving his kids or grandmother without having them protected. He made sure they had two or more. Latin King soldiers with them at all times.

"Oye, this is not like before. I not only want blood hermano. Yo necessito la poder". Don Rico said he needs the power. He shift his eyes to Little Ki Ki.

"Mira girl boy, how much is she worth to you?" Little Ki Ki fired on both of the Latin Kings having their guns pointed at Karin. The slugs crashing into their faces snapping their necks from the brute force, ejecting their brains out the other side, clearing all thoughts of bringing harm to Karin. In the same swift motion, she shift her guns on Don Rico and the other Latin King. She didn't like Don Rico's continuous disrespect or threat to Karin.

"Yo te lo dije amigo, this is not like before". Don Rico said taunting them, unphased by her shooting his goons. As those words flowed from his mouth, the female gang member Doña Tulia, was coming from behind having been in the other room, with one other Latin King soldier. Doña Tulia raising her 9mm Beretta. TK catching the movement out the corner of his eye, seeing the gun being raised to shoot Little Ki Ki in the back of the head. He reacted fast.

"Look out!" He jumped on the older woman, slapping the gun down as it went off, roaring pass Little Ki Ki's head. TK wrestled the gun away from her to no avail, when the Latin King soldier, put his gun to the back of TK's head, halting his movement or decision to fire on Doña Tulia.

"You shoot her you die next". The Latin King soldier said.

"Esperate!" Don Rico yelled out getting the soldier's attention, stopping him from doing what came natural to protect the ranking gang member.

"Say man, I'm ready to die for this shit. Just say word and these two fools is dead where they stand". Little Ki Ki said, a true street figga, honoring the code til her last breath.

"What do your bitch ass want!?" TK asked Don Rico.

"Droga, Dinero, Poder y Sangre". He wants drugs, money, power and blood.

The Latin King soldier having his finger inside of the trigger guard, ready to squeeze on Don Rico's command. Doña Tulia taking her gun from TK, pressing it to his temple.

"Oye you're valuable alive to make sure we get what we want. This puta means nada". Doña Tulia said looking at Little Ki Ki.

"She's with me til death. Just tell me what you want and it's done". TK responded being stuck in a unprepared vulnerable position. Don Rico started laughing.

"You give me the million you originally offered for that bitch that killed La Reina. Then you give me fifty kilos. Once this is done, you and your boy girl will get the fuck out of my city and state. Nobody other than Latin Kings will move and distribute product around here". Don Rico said, before pausing, nodding to the soldier, he came over by Don Rico. " Hermano we'll take her until we get the money and cocaine".

"You trippen, she ain't going anywhere. You want to take somebody, take me. I can handle myself". Little Ki Ki said, regretting this position her fiance is in. At the same time she's ready to die, if they try to take her out of this house.

Before Don Rico could respond, fast approaching sirens can be heard followed by flashing blue and red lights bouncing off of the curtains. Little Ki Ki didn't budge, she still has her Black Eagles aimed at Don Rico and his goons.

"This is my house, I can explain those two dead bodies and the rest y'all bitches if you don't leave". Little Ki Ki stated, making it clear she's about this life. Don Rico and his goons hurrying out the back door, running across the yard jumping the fence into a yard on another street escaping for now. Little Ki Ki rushed over to Karin untying her, taking the gag from her mouth. "I'm sorry Babycakes".

"I thought you were done with that shit! They came in our home, ready to kill me!" Karin cried hysterically. At the same time, the doorbell sounded off followed by a aggressive knock. She put her guns on her waistline, before turning on the 70 inch flat screen TV, with the surround sound. She headed to the front door to answer it. Opening the door, greeted by a half dozen police officers standing behind the one at the door, with their hands on their side arms.

"How are you doing today officer?" Little Ki Ki asked changing the tone of her voice.

"Someone jogging by said they heard gunshots". The officer responded.

"Not in this neighborhood. My fiance and I are watching Magnificent Seven, that's the only gunshots being heard around this respected area". She responded. Almost on cue the sounds of the gunfire on the loud surround sound can be heard followed by dialogue and music from the movie.

"I'm sorry ma'am, I mean".

"It's okay officer. It's good to know this area is safe with officers like you on duty". She said giving him a brief smile, before closing the door. She exhaled, having got this close call out of the way, not knowing what she would have done if they would have entered her home. Her guns aren't licensed. This house is now compromised. She nor Karin can stay here. When she came back into the living room, TK was wrapping the heads of these Spanish niggas with plastic bags, containing the blood spill.

"Yo good looking folk. Where Karin?" She asked.

"She ran upstairs crying. You know you can't stay here, them stupid mutha fuckas will be back. You need to build a team up here, to hold you down twenty four seven, surround yourself with trusted shooters, so shit like this don't pop off no more". TK said, pausing to secure the other body.

"I'll do what I can to make sure these Spanish niggas respect my gangsta and position of power".

"I know you going to do you. But I'm a look for them mutha fuckas, so I can gun them down one by one, for coming up in my crib sending fear through all love and care about, ya feel me?" She expressed full of anger, having slipped, allowing herself to be tracked to her crib by the Latin Kings, when she's not flashy.

Chapter 20

Three weeks passed by, TK made his way back down Atlanta. Little Ki Ki relocated, selling the house, buying a new spot in Mechanicsburg, Pennsylvania. A suburban area located twenty minutes outside of the city. White Diamond Estates, a gated community boasting homes seven thousand square feet and up. Little Ki Ki also sought the best security, hiring the Nation of Islam to protect her, Karin and their home around the clock. She was going to have the YG niggas hold her down. For now she has big plans for them. The NOI is professional, trained, serious and well groomed, fitting into this upscale area. This level of security also gave Karin comfort, after she forgave Little Ki Ki. It was easy to forgive her, especially having her own secrets, that she's holding back. What she feels for Ki Ki isn't worth the reveal of this secret. At least, not just yet, they're in a good space right now. Little Ki Ki gave Don Rico twenty five of the fifty kilos he demanded. She did it with a smile, knowing she had laced them all with high levels of fentanyl. This level of thinking, would blow back on Don Rico and all of the Latin Kings moving the product, especially when fiends snorting, shooting and smoking this tainted cocaine, started dropping, dying off. Even some of the

Latin King associates that snorted cocaine on the side, became victims of the laced product, killing them off one by one, strategically. All enhancing her position of power, while making the pressure, the presence of the drug task force and homicide detectives crackdown on all of the Latin King's territory, arresting dozens of them. All of this being made known publicly through news and social media outlets. Don Rico calling Little Ki Ki on her pre-paid cell phone number she gave him, not having any plans to further their business. She was laying bed next to Karin, who is on the computer conducting business, investing.

"What it do shawty?" Little Ki Ki answered, knowing who it is on the other end.

"Tu pinche cabron! You gave me poison!" Don Rico snapped.

"I should've killed you and that pretty bitch of yours!"

"You wanted the power. Now you got it, so deal with it. There is nothing more powerful than controlling and taking life". Little Ki Ki stated, aware that all in the hood under his command, will not be able to hustle, being labeled with a deadly product. Plus the cops is arresting all Latin Kings moving the laced cocaine, giving homicide charges for all of the bodies dropping in connection to the fentanyl tainted product. Little Ki Ki having done her research, knew it would be hard to get to Don Rico directly. With all of the Latin Kings giving him layers of protection, so she strategically wiped him and his team out, preparing for her rise and takeover. This is where the

YGs come into play, having a hundred plus members and soldiers wanting to be a part of this rising gang. Majority of its members ages twelve to seventeen. The only original YGs are in their late thirties and forties. These young goons will listen and kill without question. OG Bundles, Guru and Duttaman will lead the takeover, supplied by Little Ki Ki.

"I'm coming for you puta! You fucking girl boy! This time when I find you. I'm going to cut you into pieces and stuff all of your parts into that pretty bitches mouth ". Don Rico vented, wanting blood for this deception, that cost more Latin King lives, while placing a spotlight on his organization.

"You won't even see me coming or know that I'm the one that killed you and every one you love. I'm in control of things now. I'll take control of your entire hood, killing off the Latin King legacy and presence". She stated firmly, before ending the call, taking the battery and sim card out. Karin is now caressing Little Ki Ki's back, hearing what's going on.

"We good babe?" Karin asked.

"Yeah we good Babycakes". Karin turned the laptop screen so Little Ki Ki can see the property she just bought, a few acres of land in Philly.

"Now we need to figure out what we're going to put there". Karin said, wanting to get Ki Ki's input. Either way it's a investment worth having for Karin, especially with her vision and plans for the future.

"Office building, condos or both all in one". Ki Ki responded. Simultaneously to her answering Karin, the real business phone sounded off. She can see it's Bundles.

"Yeah man". Little Ki Ki answered.

"What up bruh? You been up on that situation on the gram and news?" Bundles asked, referring to Don Rico, the Latin Kings and tainted product. Bundles isn't aware Little Ki Ki is the mastermind behind it all, tainting the product. She's not into bragging over the jack or to anyone about this shit either. Bundles and Duttaman is only in on the takeover that he was prepared to impose, on the Ward and South Acres. Assisting in her rise to power, flooding the projects with all of their raw product and presence.

"I'm up on it. That shit all over the gram and news ya feel me. Ya folks ready to step in position, so we can lock the city down?" She responded.

"Say when, then make it right, we'll do the rest bruh". Bundles said, meaning her supplying the grade A product as promised, for the takeover which will be needed to overshadow the tainted product, luring all the fiends and heavy clientele back to the hood.

"Give it a week, then we going get it done ya hear me?"

"You already, say no more bruh". The call ended, allowing Little Ki Ki to feel the endorphins rushing through her body, rising in this game, being in this much power, while getting revenge on Don Rico's bitch ass. Especially with him evading capture from the law, being pegged as the head of the Northeast Latin King organization and supplier. Don Rico didn't realize in pursuit of respect for the crown, he loss more money and friends than expected. He even loss his position of power, that was strategically snatched from him, by a real gangsta and street figga.

Chapter 21

A few weeks later, TK was preparing to receive a new shipment from La Vieja. She increased his load to two and a half tons. Up from the one and a half ton he was getting. She figured with how fast he's been moving product, the extra ton would be more money and less trafficking back and forth with shipments coming his way. This also reduced the risk of shit happening or so they thought. TK checked his Patek Philippe no diamonds in the one of five collectors piece. He noticed the driver is now forty five minutes off schedule. He's late, and in this business dealing with this amount of product, timing is everything. Everyone must be on time and in place. When they're not, it raises red flags of things going wrong and being compromised by the law. TK sat inside of his black Brabus 500 Mercedes Benz, with tinted windows, black rims along with black interior. He was sitting across the street from his driver, that would switch vehicles with her driver picking up the load taking it to his storage. TK waited five more minutes before calling La Vieja. She picked up on the second ring, seeing who it is.

"Hola hermano, esta bien?" She asked is everything okay.

"The driver is fifty minutes late. We off schedule?" He questioned, wanting to be on the same page of business at all times. This also alerted La Vieja, who knows her driver and trail cars to protect the product left on time. "Espera un minuto hermano". She said wait a minute, while she checked, calling her goons on the other phone following the load. He picked up, immediately she can hear gunfire erupting in the background. " Que pasol?!" She asked what's going on.

"La pinched MS-13 de El Salvador!" He yelled out, making her aware they're being attacked by MS-13 gang members. They've been watching La Vieja ever since someone put them on to her. They got word through the prison system that trickled back out to the streets soldiers, to El Salvador. MS-13 gang members grew more violent once they became more violet and powerful, once they returned to their home country. Most of the gang's top command is in Chalentenango State Prison in North El Salvador. The prison only houses MS-13 gang members to keep from having deadly riots with other known violent gangs from El Salvador, like 18th Street. Both gangs far more larger and violent than the Latin Kings. La Vieja deadly as she is, is fully aware of who she's up against. "Is the package safe?" She questioned, knowing that's a lot of money to lose, even if she has it to pay or not, she's not in this game to lose like this or to be disrespected by these gang members. The goon was unable to respond to her, having been gunned down. She can hear the up close gunfire, sounding like it's coming through the phone. The MS-13 goons came six vehicles strong, cutting off the U-Haul truck from the trail cars, shooting it out with them, while the other MS-13 gang members drove up on the U-Haul truck aiming multiple guns at the driver, firing rounds on him through the passenger door, hitting the driver in the leg, arm and side, forcing him over to the side of the road. Even then, the driver knowing how vicious La Vieja is, he went out in a blaze defending the product with his life, taking the modified Tek-9 with a extended hundred round clip, squeezing unleashing a fire on the gang members, until they returned fire from all of their modified Uzi's saturating the driver's face and body with slugs, sucking the life from his flesh, before they ran up on the truck, snatching him out, pulling his lifeless bullet riddled body to the ground, before jumping in to the U-Haul taking control of the truck driving off with guns out racing off fast, followed by the six cars they came with. Back on the phone La Vieja's anger can be heard, even as she tried to remain calm and in control, having just loss two and half tons. "Hermano, something came up. There will be a delay. I'll get back to you, soon as I take care of it".

"Vieja, if you need me or my help with anything, I'm there for you". TK said showing his loyalty to her and for this business they have.

"Gracious hermano, I got it from here. I'll call you soon". She responded ending the call on fire, her jaw clenching filling with a burning rage that can only be doused with the blood of revenge in killing these gang members one by one, or going straight to the top, chopping the head off of this gangland beast who disrespected the monster she is.

La Vieja is now ready to take out all associated with the MS-13 gang, along with anyone who put them on to her load. She'll start at the top, knowing all orders of this magnitude, are given from the home country or shot callers behind bars. She'll find out who they are and wipe them all out, for even thinking they can jack her for her product. TK now having to be mindful of letting his product go for the cheap price he originally set in place under the pretense he was getting this new shipment. Everything has to change to make sure he stays ahead of this business that switches like the four seasons, and right now it's about to be a drought. He nodded to his driver that's standing by awaiting the drop.

TK gestured to him to take off, since the product isn't coming right now. The driver didn't hesitate, he jumped in the truck driving off. He got paid no matter what, for his service and code of silence, since he knows where the product is going. He wasn't stupid enough to say a word about the product's location anyway, because TK not only pays him well, he would kill him and all he values. TK drove off going in the opposite direction of his driver, heading back to his crib to work out, since he doesn't have to deal with this product, that just got jacked by the MS-13 goons.

Chapter 22

TK was driving back to his crib, when he noticed, someone following him a couple cars back. His hood instinct
heightened, senses kicking in grabbing hold of his
custom .45 Nighthawk Custom Agent 2 with the X-400
Beam on it, modified trigger, extended clip with thirty
rounds. So many thoughts running through his mind,
especially with the delayed shipment. Could it be the
Latin Kings from up north? Maybe the FBI? Either way,
it's not going to be a good day for whoever it is, since he
doesn't plan on going to jail or allowing anyone to jack
him. He turned right, passing the Exxon Mobile Gas Station. The gray Impala also turning, TK noticed, looking
into his rearview mirror. He tapped the gaspedal speeding up going around cars, trying to avoid a shootout on
this busy street, with all the strip malls, clubs and restau-
rants. His heart rate is picking up just as fast as his mind
is racing, trying to figure out his next move.

A stoplight ahead showing a yellow light. TK mashing the gas accelerating through the light, at the same
time it turned red. This dual traffic violation of speeding
and running a red light, caught the attention of a police
officer who was on the other side awaiting the light to
turn green. The officer flipping his siren and lights on,

chasing behind the fast Brabus Benz. TK now seeing this tucked the pistol before pulling over. At the same time he stopped for the police officer, the gray Impala rolled its window down as it passed by. TK having his eyes locked on the car and its driver, that's now aiming a gun at him. TK instinctively ducked down as a barrage of bullets sprayed into the car from every angle, slamming into the windows, doors hood and windshield, hitting TK in his legs, arms, side going though and through. The lone driver of the Chevy Impala is Homicide Detective Wilson from Pennsylvania, seeking revenge on TK for murdering his son and pregnant wife in cold blood. This level of violence, in his eyes didn't warrant a jail cell.

Detective Wilson went off a hunch, backed by his neighbor's description. He didn't call it in, he wanted TK's blood personally, no matter what the repercussions may be. At this point having loss all he loves in his wife and children, nothing else mattered. TK did see Detective Wilson's face. Had it not been for the cop pulling him over, he would have been prepared to shoot it out with the detective, who dumped a full clip into his car, thinking with that many shots, he had to kill TK. Detective Wilson mashed the gas racing off, at the same time the uniformed officer reacted having jumped out of the car firing on the fast fleeing Chevy Impala, before rushing over to the parked car he pulled over that's been fired on.

"Shots fired, one down! I need a medic to my location now!" The officer yelled over the radio, pumped up his adrenaline flowing.

The cop is no longer worried about the petty traffic violations. His focus is to make sure he's stable and doesn't bleed out. TK feeling the pain of the slugs, he started having his own thoughts about surviving, feeling the change in his body from the trauma of the burning slugs that breached his flesh. These thoughts and feelings made him call Red Rain who is down Cuba with Suga Baby.

"What up sexy chocolate?" Red Rain answered being playful.

"I got shot up". He responded with a strained voice.

"What!?" She questioned in and disbelief. "No, no this can't be happening!" She added.

"I'm good...I think ". He let out feeling the most pain from the slugs that went in and out. He's bleeding internally because of it.

"We'll come back now, if you want us to". Red Rain said. TK can hear the fast approaching sirens of police and ambulance coming his way. He can also see the officer from his open door directing traffic and the ambulance.

"No, I want you to be safe. I love you Shandrea. Tell Keisha I love her too". TK said. The EMTS came quick giving him medical attention. The call ended as the took him out of the car.

He still gripped the cell phone, in case he dies they'll be able to call next to kin or the last number dialed. As they took him away, all he could think about is his unborn son, Suga Baby and Red Rain. His true loves and family. This right here isn't the end he expected or how they planned it. A part of him now thinking about what La Vieja said; How life ends in this game when you're at this level. Is this my end? He's thinking. Down in Havana, Cuba Red Rain is relaying this info to Suga Baby.

"Don't trip when I tell you this. Somebody shot Tracy". Red Rain said to the now seven and half month pregnant Suga Baby. She started crying, rubbing her belly, feeling helpless fearing she could lose him. She didn't want him to be taken away from them or their son. She also felt helpless, heartbroken because she can't just up and rush back to the states being pregnant as she is, wanting to hold him down.

"I don't want to lose him Rain. We need him in our life. The baby needs him". Suga Baby cried. Red Rain comforting her, at the same time having conflicting thoughts of wanting to be in two different places at once. With TK to make sure he good, and here with Suga Baby to make sure she manage being far along in her pregnancy. Red Rain called up Little Ki Ki, to see if she can help by being present for TK.

"Say shawty what it do?" Little Ki Ki answered the phone.

"TK got shot, we can't just up and leave where we at with baby girl being pregnant right now. You think you can fly down to ATL make sure he good". Red Rain asked.

"I'm on it soon as we hang up shawty. Tell lil mama I got this, don't stress that baby out, ya feel me?" Little Ki

Ki responded, being loyal to the team that put her in a position to be as rich and powerful as she is now.

"Call me when you get to ATL".

"You already know. Keep ya mind clear and lil mama in comfort. I got this ya feel me?" She said ending the call, taking a private jet from JETASAP.COM, flying with the licensed NOI security.

Chapter 23

A few hours later, Little Ki Ki's private jet landed at the airport in Atlanta. Two Yukon Denalis awaiting her and the NOI security, taking them to the hospital she discovered TK is at. Little Ki Ki now wondering why TK didn't have security with him, being in the position of power he's in, especially after that incident at her old crib with Don Rico. She wasn't about to let that shit happen to her again or allow any harm to come to Karin, who has four of her own NOI security at the house with her now, coupled with the Brinks Alarm system. The presence of these trained men, gives her and Ki Ki the comfort and peace of mind. As the trucks drove off heading to hospital, Ki Ki is taking in the city she left behind. The city that started her off in this business. Now she's in a position to look back to the hood if need be. Although she missed Atlanta, she got a lot of love from up north, especially the YG niggas from Harrisburg.

While the Denalis are heading to the hospital, Detective Wilson not realizing the Atlanta PD, after looking at the dash camera, running the tags on the car he was driving has linked it to him and the hotel room he booked. They raided the room to no avail, he was just entering the hospital after finding out he didn't kill TK. He made his way to the receptionist, flashing his Pennsylvania Detective Badge.

"Homicide, I'm looking for a shooting victim, Tracy King". Detective Wilson said calmly, like he's on then job working the case. The female behind the counter running her fingers across the keyboard, punching in the name he just gave her. The Atlanta PD not wanting his real name listed after the discovery of Detective Wilson being the shooter.

"We don't have a Tracy King. You said he was shot?" She questioned, needing him to be more specific. He was looking around seeming anxious, pumped with adrenaline, ready to finish what he started. Not giving a fuck about Tracy 'TK' King or being a homicide detective. All that shit went out of the window, the moment he discovered his family butchered with a knife, ripping a part of him into pieces, emotionally and mentally.

"How many John Does do you have that came in here, within the last few hours?" He asked, thinking like homicide detective, instead of someone who simply wanting to commit murder to appease the burning rage inside of him.

"Okay, that's much better". She said punching it in.

"We have two that came in as John Does, both shot multiple times. Sixth floor, rooms six twenty and six zero four". She responded.

Hearing this made him excited with a dose of adrenaline and thoughts of finishing TK off. The rush of murdering is racing through his body and mind. He hurried to the elevator, getting inside pressing the button to the sixth floor. As the elevator doors are closing Little Ki Ki and her six NOI security team came through the front door, making their way straight to the row of elevators, already knowing TK's room number. Detective Wilson taking a deep breath as the elevator doors opened to the sixth floor. He looked both ways to find the numerical order of the rooms the receptionist gave him. He went to room six zero four first, seeing two officers outside of the room talking to one another. Detective Wilson came up flashing his badge quick.

"Homicide, is our guy coming around?" He asked trying to get a glimpse into the room, seeing a older woman and a teen girl at the bed side crying.

"This guy may not make it, with as many bullets he caught in the back trying to run from the stick up boys in the projects". The officer said. Detective Wilson knowing now this isn't the room.

"The mindset of these kids, not wanting to work, they'd rather sell drugs, rob and kill one another". Detective Wilson said before walking away, taking long strides to room six twenty, where he can see one officer outside of the room, the other chair empty.

"Homicide, where's your partner?" Detective Wilson asked like he's familiar with the officers.

"He had a few bad tacos sir, so he ran to the restroom". The officer responded.

"This is going to be a long night, get me a triple black coffee, get yourself one too". Detective Wilson said, handing the officer a ten dollar bill. Little Ki Ki and the NOI security is turning into the hallway leading to the room, seeing the police officer walking away as the Homicide Detective Wilson entered the room, removing his side arm.

His adrenaline spiking through his body, approaching the unconscious TK, who is medicated after the surgery to remove the bullets from his body that were lodged in his leg close to a main artery. A half a centimeter to the right, he would have never made it to the hospital alive. Detective Wilson snatched out the morphine drip out of TK's arm.

"I want you to feel all of this pain mutha fucka!" He said, squeezing the trigger firing a round into TK's stomach abruptly awaking him, feeling this compromise to his body being breached violently. At the same time this roaring round was fired, the NOI security moved quick removing their guns racing towards the room. The two officers outside of the other room radioing in, while running behind the NOI security. TK's eyes wide open, realizing his end is near.

"How could you be so heartless killing my son and pregnant wife!?" Detective Wilson snapped, taking his gun pressing it into the fresh wound, inflicting pain on TK.

"Agggggh!!" TK let out.

"That's what I want you to feel before death mutha fucka!" Detective Wilson stated, shifting his weapon towards TK's face.

Right then, the trained NOI soldiers entered the room fanning out, firing immediately on the threat to human life, which is Detective Wilson. Each trained NOI security hitting the heart, killing Detective Wilson, halting all thoughts he had of torturing and murdering TK.

"Put your hands up!" The officers running behind said. "We have license to carry and protect our clients. This man needs medical attention now, he's been shot by the one on the floor". The NOI security said, taking out their security credentials and license. Ki Ki rushing over to TK.

"I got you folk. Sorry I couldn't beat this bitch ass nigga here, he dead now". Little Ki Ki said.

The nurses came in fast rushing over to TK securing him before transferring to surgery to remove the bullet in his stomach. TK couldn't believe this shit is happening to him, twice in the same day, by the same crazy ass cop, trying to avenge his family. Is this the power you seek? TK flashed back to the night he stood before La Reina the powerful Latin Queen, when she asked him and Suga Baby this in their pursuit to take over. Never did he ever think it would be like this. He started to rethink it all as he slipped in and out of consciousness, going to surgery. Little Ki Ki hired NOI security for TK, even if he thought he didn't need it, he'll have it now. She didn't plan on leaving Atlanta until he got better. Karin understood with her being close to TK. It also gave Karin time to focus on business and visit family she hasn't seen in awhile. Ki Ki also reached out to Red Rain, letting her know she's in the A. Also to put her on to that unexpected shit that popped off, trying to kill TK.

"Ki Ki, we can't stay stuck here so far away from y'all and all that's going on". Red Rain said, wanting to be close to TK to nurse him back to health with love and affection.

"Say shawty, you may be good coming back, but think about lil mamma totting the baby, it's a lot on her right now, ya feel me?" Ki Ki responded.

"When TK comes out of surgery, I want you to have him face time us". She said worrying about him. Wanting to see him with his eyes open, so she can be in comfort knowing he's okay.

"Everything is going be good shawty, I promise on my life ya hear me?"

"Yeah I hear you. Just tell him we love and miss him. We love you too Ki Ki".

"You already know what it is". She said hanging up, embracing being the temporary east coast boss.

The Crown Is Mine

Chapter 24

Two weeks later, TK was back at the house with six new NOI security in and around his home. Little Ki Ki also stuck around after La Vieja contacted TK to send another load through, that was also intercepted, cutting off supply that is now much needed to secure the east coast. This interception alerted La Vieja that someone inside her organization must have tipped MS-13 off to this, so she used her resources tracking those close to her aware of the distribution times. She found out who the mole is, so she kept a close watch on him, along with scheduling a fake shipment drop, with a dozen Mexican goons in the back of the U-Haul, jumping out on the MS-13 gang members, gunning them down, only taking one alive to extract info. Then they called La Vieja up. She was in a meeting with members of her inner circle, when the call came in.

"Hola Que tal?" She asked.

"Senora, esta hecho". The soldier making her aware that it's done.

"You know where to go and what to do. I'll be there soon". She responded hanging up, shifting her attention to the men and women in the room. "Everyone in this room hungers for more money. Some of us even yearn for power, mi poder". She said they want her power. She came over to the Mexican associate that was in control of distribution. The one who flies to Mexico securing the product, shipping it to the Miami ports. He's also responsible on her command, to direct the product up and down the east coast. His name, Miguel Vasquez, born in Sinaloa, Mexico. A stone cold killer and business-man. La Vieja removing the hair pin, letting her silky hair down as she continued to speak. "I put you all in position to feed your families. To secure a future for generations, yet in return I get betrayal". She said nodding her head to her Mexican security goons. They moved quick snatch-ing Miguel up, even then he tried to go for his weapon, with no luck. They secured his gun as she came up on him, staring into his eyes with a dark murderous look.

"Tu quieres mi poder?" She asked if he wants her power.

"No, no lo siento Vieja". He's vehemently denying his actions apologizing, realizing he's cornered and caught. Now she'll not only kill him, but all he loves to assure there is no retaliation later on down the line, in her pur-suit stay in power. She took the weaponized hairpin that's razor sharp, slamming it into his heart, staring intently into his eyes, then she abruptly turned the sharp blade, sealing his fate. He let out a gasp feeling his life escaping his flesh. She turned to the others in the room, each of them understanding what just took place needed to happen to assure respect, loyalty and her position of power. Miguel's family would also be killed off because of his disloyal behavior.

"Everyone here is excused. I have business to tend to". La Vieja said, before she too exited with her team of goons, heading over to the backside of the plaza she owns, where a storage area is. It's also where her Mexican goons held the tortured and beaten MS-13 member that tried to jack her load. When she entered the MS-13 member could tell who she is from her presence amongst the men that guarded her. The look in her eyes along with the way she conducted herself, displaying the power he's heard of. MS-13 is known to terrorize El Salvador and all in their way. They're also contracted killers, known to leave behind a bloody massacre.

"Where's my product?" She questioned. Her level of violence is needed knowing the cartel boss Hector, doesn't tolerate excuses when it comes to his money or product.

"It doesn't matter. They're not going to give it back to you because you know where it is, they're lives will protect it". The MS-13 member responded trying to be tough honoring his gang.

"Let me worry about getting this product back, just tell me where it is". She said blowing smoke into his face, then added. "I will have these men peel your skin slowly from your flesh, until you beg to die, if you don't tell me where my product is". She stated firmly, allowing him to see the darkness of death in her eyes.

"Little Havana, but not for long, they found a buyer". He blurted out hoping to evade a gruesome death of being skinned alive.

He volunteered the exact location and more. She also squeezed out of him, who sanctioned this attack. Even with the inside direction to the product from Miguel, they needed MS-13 ranking command to authorize this. She discovered it's a boss in El Salvador at Chalentenango, a state prison. Auturo Velagez, a violent goon that spent ten years in Lewisburg Federal Penitentiary on the maximum side, before being extradited to El Salvador, where his rank and power over the most violent gang in Central America, grew even more.

"Your gang may be violent, but you are all stupid to fuck with me. Now I'll show you all what power looks like". She said taking her cigarette putting it out in his eye. He screamed in pain never feeling nothing like this.

"Aaagggh! Ahi Dios Mio!"

"You're going to need more than God. Oye mata lo". She said giving the order to kill him.

Her goons taking a thin metal wire, wrapping it around his neck, twisting it using a short stick, constricting his air making him convulse in search of much needed oxygen. The wire even cut deep into his flesh, adding pain on top of suffocation.The MS-13 goon now shaking violently wanting to get air, wanting to live, then it got dark as his life fled his body. La Vieja never turning away, staring in his eyes wanting to see this piece of shit's life leave his body.

Once she was done here, she gave the order for her Mexican goons she brought in from Juarez, Mexico to take out all present protecting the product that belongs to her, then bring her back the tons they stole. She paid them a million cash for their gangland style services. She also set in place a hit on the top MS-13 bosses, to make sure this doesn't happen again. Everyone in this business will respect her gangsta.

148

The Crown Is Mine

Chapter 25

A few days later, La Vieja had simultaneous operations in America and in El Salvador, hitting the top two MS-13 bosses that were incarcerated. The American boss is locked up in Marion Federal Penitentiary. He was hit in the yard, that turned into a riot with other MS-13 gang members all joining the cutting, stabbing and slashing fest, even when the tower guards shot smoke grenades into the yard. The CERT team came fast suited up, taking down all that isn't face down on the ground. The special response team using rubber bullets, stun shields, tasers and pepper spray, taking down each gang member, even those still gripping their shanks with blood dripping from it. Down in El Salvador at the state prison Chalentenango, MS-13 Don and shot caller of the organization, Auturo Velagez was in his cell with a few others, drinking, smoking while getting new gang tattoos. Some honoring close associates, others paying respect to the family members that died. One of Auturo's paid correctional officers came in with a package from the U. S., he opened it seeing a cell phone, with a typed note that read: Llamame ahora! He did just that, stopping the hommie from tattooing him.

"Espera hermano, I have to make this call". Auturo said calling the preprogrammed number.

"Hola Que tal Auturo?" La Vieja said feeling good that he took the call, setting in place her next move.

"Quien es ese?" He asked who is it?

"La pesidilla para ti". She responded that she's a nightmare for him.

"Tu pinche cabrona!" He snapped calling her a fucking bitch.

"You fucked with the wrong bitch, estupido". She said tapping in a code on her phone sending a signal to the phone he's holding.

Right then, the needles she had installed filled with tetrodotoxin a poisonous and deadly neurotoxin, found in Puffer fish. It came out fast sticking into his hand. The fast acting poison, halting all normal responses, to jump, release or shout out in pain, only grunting. His body seem to freeze in place as the injected poison raced through his veins, reaching and shutting down all of his internal organs, and brain. Making him suffocate, unable to find breath or help to save his life, he so much wanted right now. He should have thought of this before he chose to sanction a robbery against America's most violent female cartel figure in the underground business.

The MS-13 jacking wasting her time, also placing a brighter spotlight on her from the feds, due to the level of violence that has occurred in the wake of the MS-13 taking her tons of cocaine. If Budda was still living, he would have been able to relay this information to her. Now she'll have to deal with it, if they come her way. For now, her main focus is boosting security around her, all of the shipments including her children and those close to her. Especially with her having put the hit out on the two shot callers of MS-13, sending a message not to fuck with her. A message she wanted the third world vicious MS-13 gang members to respect her gangsta knowing she can reach all of them at any time.

La Vieja knowing the only way to hurt them, is to kill who they look up to. She did just that from the position of power she haves. After she took out the two shot callers, she stared directing product up and down the east coast and Midwest, through TK and his team. TK is healing up one day at a time, with Nurse Sabrina looking after him, along with the NOI securing him and his home, while Ki Ki is holding him down running the business as the other east coast boss under La Vieja. Ki Ki made it back up north to be with her sexy fiance Karin, wanting to give her the world for her loyalty and patience. Suga Baby and Red Rain also contemplating on coming back to the states, not wanting anything else to happen without them being present to help. They also figured with Detective Wilson gone, no one would be looking for Suga Baby. Truthfully, the two of them would find any excuse to be a family with TK.

Chapter 26

Seven months passed by, La Vieja's position of power secured, shutting down any attempts on her life, in retaliation from MS-13, having a new shot caller vowing to avenge Auturo Velagez. Each attempt was met with dozens of MS-13 gang members meeting their graphic demise cartel style. Now controlling half of the United States, her position of power has grown. TK, Suga Baby, Red Rain are all now living under one roof. A family, as each of them envisioned. All of them loving every memory being made with their son, while staying in control of the game that's making them plenty of money. Ki Ki now having expanded out the Midwest further up north, along with West Virginia, and Virginia. Ki Ki ran into a situation with the Mendez twins, who's getting their cocaine from a cartel boss out of Tijuana. He goes by the name Padrino, meaning the Godfather. Ki Ki being a mastermind in this business that's strategic at this level. She employed the Vice Lords, and Gangsta Disciples, to assure the takeover of Chicago. By giving them better prices and higher quality product. This thought out move, halted the Mendez brothers income and distribution, angering them with this loss of income and respect from gangs that purchased large quantities of product. The Mendez brothers, now getting pressure from their boss back home in Mexico, wanting them to off the product he's fronting them, so money will be made and sent back to Tijuana. Padrino didn't care about the American that's trying to under cut them, he wanted his money for all the product he sent to the states. The twins knowing they're in need of this distribution or they would be no good to the cartel connect, meaning it would be the end of business by way of their demise. Ki Ki on the other hand, didn't care about the Mendez twins problem, they would have to change cities and states, because she's running shit over this way right now. Ki Ki should know with growth comes power, exposure, envy and haters. All eyes are on Ki Ki, Red Rain, TK and Suga Baby, who are all actively running a multimillion dollar cocaine empire, thanks to the queen bitch herself, La Vieja. La Vieja wanting to show her appreciation to TK and his team for all the millions they've made her, so she booked a trip to Nassau, Bahamas for a vacation. They were all on Paradise Island on the white sand beach living their best lives, far away from the streets they grew up in, getting their start in the game from the block to the top. Suga Baby now fit looking like she never even had a child, wearing her red bikini showing her curves off with the beads of water racing over her flesh as she exited the aqua blue waters along side of Red Rain who's wearing a light blue bikini with water racing over her body of perfection. Each of them looking sexy like they're shooting a music video. They made their way over to the paid baby sitter that's looking after Junior while the adults are enjoying the beach life here on Paradise Island.

"Junior still sleeping?" Suga Baby asked the baby sitter.

"Yes, he's having his own little vacation". The sitter responded.

"Look at his dad acting crazy". Red Rain said seeing TK picked La Vieja up out of the water, carrying her before letting her down. She's wearing a white bikini looking very fit for her age. TK also healed and still in shape, showing off his fit frame with the scars from this gangsta boss life he lives. Ki Ki is wearing a Nike sports bra with black swim trunks. She's playing with Karin splashing water in her face before embracing her with affectionate kisses in between palming her ass, sliding her fingers under her pink bikini, showing off her body of a goddess. The NOI security along with La Vieja's goons secured the beach area where they are, allowing them to enjoy this vacation in comfort without looking over their shoulders.

"This is the life right here". TK said as he and La Vieja headed back to their beach side chairs to enjoy their frozen drinks.

"You deserve it hermano. You've come a long way from the confines of prison to Paradise Island". La Vieja said now sitting down sipping her frozen pinacolada the server just brought over to them at their request after they're done in the water.

"What's crazy, I had my mind set to take over the city I left in power. Shit played out different, good and bad.

Overall I'm loving my new life, friends and family". TK said looking over at Suga Baby and Red Rain. Each of them always desiring him sexually, loving all he brings into their lives.

"We're all family now hermano. I know without question you will ride and die for me, as you Americans say. As you know I'll do the same and more if need be". La Vieja said.

"To family and staying in power ". TK said raising his frozen drink tapping her glass.

"Familia y poder". She repeated, before sipping her frozen drink.

Suddenly, Ki Ki yelling out getting their attention.

"Aye yo! Look at them speed boats coming this way folk". Ki Ki said standing there on the beach with her hand on Karin's soft ass, looking over at her NOI security who is already on point walking towards the beach, seeing the fast approaching boats aren't slowing down.

Who could it be? Wild tourists? A hit? They didn't care, they're all here to do a job, protecting their clients. La Vieja's goons also joined the NOI security, only two of her goons stayed close by behind her.

The server also looking at the fast approaching boats, noticing the men and women are wearing FBI jackets. The server leaned over to La Vieja. " Can I help you with anything else?" She asked. For the first time La Vieja is registering this young female looking to be eighteen is not a native of the island, her original accent was fake. La Vieja also seeing for the first time, the MS-13 tattoo on her neck that was covered by her collar. Unable to react as fast as the young teen, who blew out a razor from her mouth, slicing the razor deep across La Vieja's throat, cutting her windpipe, severing a main artery in her neck.

"Es para Auturo Velagez, MS-13 siempre puta!" The young gang member said. In the same swift motion, La Vieja's goons removed their side arms gunning down the MS-13 gang member, unleashing multiple rounds dropping her, even standing over top of her firing rounds into her face. Suga Baby and Red Rain securing TK junior, shielding him from violence or bullets if anymore were to follow behind this unexpected hit, disregarding the fast approaching FBI.

The FBI agents boats rushing into shallow waters, before they jumped off the boats with their badges and jackets visible of who they are. Guns out at the ready. The NOI put their side arms away seeing there's more federal agents came from behind them out of the woods on the island.

"You're all under arrest for trafficking and distribution!" The federal agents yelled out, closing in on all of them. TK looking over at La Vieja slumped in the chair with blood spewing from her neck. He couldn't believe this is all happening. Karin is crying hysterically being cuffed along with Ki Ki, who is pissed.

"My baby! Please don't take my baby from me!" Suga Baby yelled out crying, as they removed her son from her grasp only to put handcuffs on her. The agents handing her son to the baby sitter, while they secured the ones they came for.

TK is feeling like he let them down, not being able to protect them as he always promised to do. As much as they wanted to be family, they should have stayed in Cuba. When they came back, he was just as happy to see them as they were of him. In that moment it all felt right. Even worst now with La Vieja being murdered in cold blood, cutting the head off of the operation, leaving him to be the one they tag as the boss. The power they all sought, left a lot of people pissed off who envied and hated on them. The same people willing to give the FBI information needed to take down this monstrous organization, that controlled over seventy percent of cocaine flowing into America, flooding the streets. As the FBI is hauling them off they're all realizing this good life at the top, has come to an end. They didn't get a chance to shoot it out as they all once thought and talked about. Now they're going to jail to fight a federal beef with the evidence the FBI has that lead to this moment right here. The one person the FBI wanted the most, they didn't get, she's laying with her throat cut open, dead with her blood saturating the white sands. TK looking on at La Vieja's lifeless body wishing he could have prevented it, gunning down that little bitch that got at her. He shook his head before turning to look on at his ride or die females including Lil Ki Ki, being cuffed and hauled away.

"Yo y'all can let them go. Anything y'all got you can pin that shit on me!" TK said to the FBI agents escorting him to the boats. "Keisha! Shandrea, Ki Ki! I love all of y'all. Don't worry I'm a make this shit right. I wanted the crown, so I'm a wear it to the grave". He said standing firm, ready to take the fall for all charges, so Red Rain and Suga Baby can live out their lives raising junior, loving one another. He also want Little Ki Ki and Karin to live out their best life. He knows no matter what, he wouldn't want for anything, his loyalty is love. Their loyalty and respect for him is all love. He didn't trip, only accepting the fate of what's to come of this prison sentence the feds will hit him with. Even then, he'll remain a king wearing the crown he chased from the day he came home from upstate with no regrets and no mercy on anyone in the way of his rise to power. He'll without question be honoring the code of the game and streets, as long as he's breathing.

GOOD 2 GO PUBLISHING CATALOG ORDER FORM

To order books, please fill out the order form below (Please allow up to 2 weeks for shipping)
Make checks payable to: Good2Go Publishing P.O Box 758, Laveen, AZ 85339

Name: _____ Address: _____ City: _____

State: _____ Zip Code: _____ Phone: _____ Email: _____

Item Name	Price	Qty	Amnt	Item Name	Price	Qty	Amnt
48 Hours to Die – Silk White	$15.00			My Brothers Envy 3 – J. L. Rose	$15.00		
A Hustler's Dream – Ernest Morris	$15.00			Naughty Housewives – Ernest Morris	$15.00		
A Hustler's Dream 2 – Ernest Morris	$15.00			Naughty Housewives 2 – Ernest Morris	$15.00		
A Thug's Devotion – J.L. Rose	$15.00			Naughty Housewives 3 – Ernest Morris	$15.00		
Affliction – Assa Raymond Baker	$15.00			Naughty Housewives 4 – Ernest Morris	$15.00		
Affliction 2 – Assa Raymond Baker	$15.00			Never Be The Same – Silk White	$15.00		
All Eyes on Gunz – Warren Holloway	$15.00			Scarred Knuckles – Raymond Baker	$15.00		
All Eyes on Gunz 2 – Warren Holloway	$15.00			Scarred Knuckles 2 – Raymond Baker	$15.00		
All Eyes on Gunz 3 – Warren Holloway	$15.00			Secrets in the Dark Ernest Morris	$15.00		
All Eyes on Gunz 4 – Warren Holloway	$15.00			Shades of Revenge – Assa Raymond Baker	$15.00		
Betrayal Within – Ernest Morris	$15.00			Shoebox Money – Warren Holloway	$15.00		
Black Reign – Ernest Morris	$15.00			Slumped – Jason Brent	$15.00		
Bloody Mayhem Down South – Trayvon Jackson	$15.00			Someone's Gonna Get It – Mychea	$15.00		
Bloody Mayhem Down South 2 – Trayvon Jackson	$15.00			Stranded – Silk White	$15.00		
Business Is Business – Silk White	$15.00			Supreme & Justice – Ernest Morris	$15.00		
Business Is Business 2 – Silk White	$15.00			Supreme & Justice 2 – Ernest Morris	$15.00		
Business Is Business 3 – Silk White	$15.00			Supreme & Justice 3 – Ernest Morris	$15.00		
Cash In Cash Out – Assa Raymond Baker	$15.00			Sweet Peas Tough Choices – Silk White	$15.00		
Cash In Cash Out 2 – Assa Raymond Baker	$15.00			Tears of a Hustler – Silk White	$15.00		
Chi City Boyz – Asia Hill	$15.00			Tears of a Hustler 2 – Silk White	$15.00		
Childhood Sweethearts – Jacob Spears	$15.00			Tears of a Hustler 3 – Silk White	$15.00		
Childhood Sweethearts 2 – Jacob Spears	$15.00			Tears of a Hustler 4– Silk White	$15.00		
Childhood Sweethearts 3 – Jacob Spears	$15.00			Tears of a Hustler 5 – Silk White	$15.00		
Childhood Sweethearts 4 – Jacob Spears	$15.00			Tears of a Hustler 6 – Silk White	$15.00		
Connected To The Plug – Dwan Williams	$15.00			The Excitement I Bring – Warren Holloway	$15.00		
Connected To The Plug 2 – Dwan Williams	$15.00			The Excitement I Bring 2 – Warren Holloway	$15.00		
Connected To The Plug 3 – Dwan Williams	$15.00			The Last Love Letter – Warren Holloway	$15.00		
Connected To The Plug 4 – Dwan Williams	$15.00			The Last Love Letter 2 – Warren Holloway	$15.00		
Connected to the Plug 4 – Dwan Williams	$15.00			The Panty Ripper – Reality Way	$15.00		
Cost of Betrayal – Warren Holloway	$15.00			The Panty Ripper 3 – Reality Way	$15.00		
Cost of Betrayal 2 – Warren Holloway	$15.00			The Serial Cheater – Silk White	$15.00		
Death by Association – Ernest Morris	$15.00			The Solution – J. M. Morrison	$15.00		
Death by Association 2 – Ernest Morris	$15.00			The Teflon Queen – Silk White	$15.00		
Dreams Life – Assa Raymond Baker	$15.00			The Teflon Queen 2 – Silk White	$15.00		
Dreams Life 2 – Assa Raymond Baker	$15.00			The Teflon Queen 3 – Silk White	$15.00		
Flipping Numbers – Ernest Morris	$15.00			The Teflon Queen 4 – Silk White	$15.00		
Flipping Numbers 2 – Ernest Morris	$15.00			The Teflon Queen 5 – Silk White	$15.00		
Forbidden Pleasure – Ernest Morris	$15.00			The Teflon Queen 6 – Silk White	$15.00		
He Loves Me, He Loves You Not – Mychea	$15.00			The Vacation – Silk White	$15.00		
He Loves Me, He Loves You Not 2 – Mychea	$15.00			Tied to a Boss – J. L. Rose	$15.00		
He Loves Me, He Loves You Not 3 – Mychea	$15.00			Tied to a Boss 2 – J. L. Rose	$15.00		
He Loves Me, He Loves You Not 4 – Mychea	$15.00			Tied to a Boss 3 – J. L. Rose	$15.00		
He Loves Me, He Loves You Not 5 – Mychea	$15.00			Tied to a Boss 4 – J. L. Rose	$15.00		
Healing In The Midst of Adversity –Michelle Murray	$15.00			Tied to a Boss 5 – J. L. Rose	$15.00		
Killing Signs – Ernest Morris	$15.00			Time Is Money – Silk White	$15.00		
Killing Signs 2 – Ernest Morris	$15.00			Tomorrow's Not Promised – Robert Torres	$15.00		
King of the Night – Warren Holloway	$15.00			Tomorrow's Not Promised 2 – Robert Torres	$15.00		
Kings of the Block – Dwan Williams	$15.00			Trapped in Love – Ernest Morris	$15.00		
Kings of the Block 2 – Dwan Williams	$15.00			Two Mask One Heart – Jacob Spears & Trayvon Jackson	$15.00		
Lord of My Land – J.M. Morrison	$15.00			Two Mask One Heart 2 – Jacob Spears & Trayvon Jackson	$15.00		
Lost and Turned Out – Ernest Morris	$15.00			Two Mask One Heart 3 – Jacob Spears & Trayvon Jackson	$15.00		
Love and Basketball – J.L. Rose	$15.00			Wife – Raneissa Baker	$15.00		
Love and Deception – Warren Holloway	$15.00			Wife 2 – Raneissa Baker	$15.00		
Love Hates Violence – De'Wayne Maris	$15.00			Wrong Place Wrong Time – Silk White	$15.00		
Love Hates Violence 2 – De'Wayne Maris	$15.00			Young Goonz – Reality Way	$15.00		
Love Hates Violence 3 – De'Wayne Maris	$15.00			Secrets in the Dark 2 – Ernest Morris (New Release)	$15.00		
Love Hates Violence 4 – De'Wayne Maris	$15.00			Secrets in the Dark 1 – Ernest Morris (New release)	$15.00		
Loyalty to a Gangsta – J.L. Rose	$15.00			The Danger That Lurks Within – Ernest Morris	$15.00		
Married To Da Streets – Silk White	$15.00			When Love Happens – Warren Holloway	$15.00		
Mercenary in Love – J.L. Rose	$15.00			The Unexpected – Warren	$15.00		
Mercenary in Love 2 – J.L. Rose	$15.00			Finding Her Love – Warren Holloway	$15.00		
My Besties – Asia Hill	$15.00			Murder and Deception – Warren Holloway	$15.00		
My Besties 2 – Asia Hill	$15.00			Entanglement – Raymond Baker	$15.00		
My Besties 3 – Asia Hill	$15.00			The Crown Is Mine. Part I	$15.00		
My Besties 4 – Asia Hill	$15.00			The Crown Is Mine. Part II	$15.00		
My Boyfriend's Wife – Mychea	$15.00			The Crown Is Mine. Part III	$15.00		
My Boyfriend's Wife 2 – Mychea	$15.00			NOTE: Please make sure the books you order are accepted we are not responsible for rejected orders.			
My Brothers Envy – J. L. Rose	$15.00			Total: Shipping (Free) Us Media Mail			
My Brothers Envy 2 – J. L. Rose	$15.00						

www.ingramcontent.com/pod-product-compliance
Lightning Source LLC
Chambersburg PA
CBHW071223260626
47162CB00004B/1410